"I recall a daughter, though I am afraid it has been many years since I've thought of her. I cannot remember her name."

"Margaret. Or perhaps you knew her as Meg."

"Oh, yes. That's it. Meg. We spent some time together right here. Well, upstairs in the nursery."

"Then we are likely already acquainted, too."

"I don't recall meeting someone like you," she began, her frown growing as she peered at him. "Unless…"

"Hector," he supplied, and then smiled as she appeared to recognize his name.

But her eyes had narrowed upon him. "Oh, it's you."

HEATHER BOYD

USAT BESTSELLING AUTHOR

Silver BELLS

◆

Distinguished Rogues

17

The characters and events portrayed in this book are fictitious. Any similarity to real persons, living or dead, is purely coincidental and not intended by the author.

SILVER BELLS © 2020 by Heather Boyd
ISBN: 978-1-925239-82-9
Editing by Kelli Collins

Chapter One

RUBY ROPER SHIVERED at the sudden chill of the kitchen and wished she were outside in the real cold of a snowy field. "What do you mean, I'm leaving?"

Her father-in-law sniffed. "Fergus Masters requires a wife and likes the look of you, despite everything."

Despite Ruby being English is what he meant. Mr. Roper, a Scotsman with an unrelenting dislike for anyone born English, had never approved his son's choice of bride. He now made no bones about how worthless she was to the family since his son was no longer alive to defend her existence.

Ruby was considered a burden. The fact that she had loved their son from the moment they'd met until he'd suddenly passed away a year ago counted for nothing in Mr. Roper's eyes. Nor did the dowry she'd brought to the marriage. That money had disappeared into the family coffers, never to be seen again.

Now, a year after she'd buried Liam Roper, his father would be rid of her. "I don't know the man well enough to consider such an alliance."

"Well, ya canna stay here," he said, rising to tower over Ruby at his dinner table. "It's him, or you'll find your way in the world. He'll be here tomorrow."

Ruby swallowed. "To meet us?"

"To fetch you, girlie. I'll have none of your fancy talk of long courtships. You wrapped our Liam around your finger. Keeping him away from his duty to the family for too long." Mr. Roper jabbed a finger in her direction. "You'll tie the knot without a fuss, as every other Scottish lass does, and be grateful I thought of you at all."

She shivered at the future her father-in-law had in store for her. But it made her decision to leave next week, return home to the family she'd become estranged from, all the more urgent. She didn't have a week to escape with her son. "You can't possibly want to send Pip away from the only home he's ever known."

Mr. Roper shook his head. "The boy stays with us. He belongs here."

Ruby stood. "No, I won't be parted from Pip."

Roper raised his hand above her face, ready to strike her. "You'll do as ya told, lass."

She trembled, waiting for the blow…but it never came. Her mother-in-law had taken hold of her husband's elbow and stopped him.

"Not in my kitchen," Eliza Roper cried out.

Mr. Roper threw off his wife's grip and turned away. He went to his grandson and ordered Pip up on his feet. Ruby's son was only four, with hardly any idea what was going on. He faced his grandfather with a smile. "Can we go to the stables and see my papa's horse?"

"Aye, lad. We're done here," Mr. Roper announced.

When they left the room, Ruby nearly cried. Roper was a hard man who'd never had need to punish her child, but she feared what he would do to her little boy.

Ruby swallowed hard. She'd run away this minute if she had the fare. Her original plan was to take the mail coach back to cross the border into England and make her way south as fast as she could. But she still had days of work to go on a piece of embroidery that she would sell to pay for the journey. Getting there without funds would be an impossible trip with a young child.

Ruby had never had a fair chance to make a place for herself within Liam's family. They'd never tried to accept her the way they did her four-year-old son, Pip. As the only male grandchild, he'd been beloved since birth. And for weeks now, her father-in-law had been attempting to keep them apart in subtle ways.

But it seemed Mr. Roper was done being subtle. Fergus Masters lived many miles away, a relative of one of their neighbors who had visited recently. She could not imagine she would ever be allowed to see her son again once she was moved away.

The silence left in Mr. Roper's wake was deafening, and Ruby finally looked at her mother-in-law when she sat opposite. Eliza Roper stared at her steadily, and then she shook her head. "You'll be Fergus' fourth wife. His last wife died along with the third daughter she bore him."

Ruby swallowed hard.

She had never been sure how Eliza thought

of her. She'd offered Ruby very little kindness over the years they'd shared the upkeep of this house. But Eliza had not been entirely without compassion over the past five years. She'd taken charge of Ruby's lying in and delivered Pip safely into Ruby's arms. However, Eliza always sided with her husband. She'd adored her son while he'd lived, but her grandson Pip had become the center of her world. When Ruby was married off, no doubt she would take over raising young Pip in his grandfather's image.

"You canna stay, lass," Eliza informed her.

"I loved your son. He wouldn't want this for Pip or me." Ruby stood and began clearing the table angrily. She could expect no help from Eliza. The woman was Mr. Roper's puppet, too.

Eliza sighed. "I know you did, and he loved you, but he's dead now, and you've got to think of the future."

Ruby carried everything into the kitchens. Roper had funds to pay for a maid to do the work, but he was too tight-fisted to pay anyone properly. In the end, it was left to Eliza and Ruby to keep the house tidy. Ruby had taken on the lion's share of the work to spare her mother-in-law from scrubbing her fingers raw in the hope of becoming friends.

The work of filling the sinks took some time, and her mother-in-law watched her work without comment as she often did.

Ruby finished and turned.

Eliza was holding out Ruby's secret bit of

embroidery. The piece she meant to sell to escape Scotland.

Ruby wet her lips. "Where did you get that?"

"Ye canna keep secrets in my 'ouse," Eliza warned. She turned it over. "It's not finished."

"No."

Eliza suddenly tucked the piece into the bodice of her gown. "Mine now."

"No, please!" Ruby cried. "Give it back to me."

Ruby had hoarded that linen and thread since the day she'd left home. If Eliza took it, she'd have nothing of any real value left.

"It's not finished, and you won't have time." Eliza went to the kitchen hearth and crouched down. She moved a log of wood, and then turned back to Ruby. "You need to leave," Eliza repeated. When she approached Ruby, she held a tiny pile of coins in her hand. "Go to your family."

"I will not leave my son behind."

"I expected nothing less." Eliza grabbed Ruby's hand, uncurled her fingers, and started counting out coins into Ruby's palm until she had enough for the fare and food on the journey home to England for both her and Pip too.

Ruby gaped, stunned. She had to stop her when it became too much. "I don't know what to say."

"You raise him right, teach him what he needs to know about his father and his family. Give him the education his father would want

Pip to have. You send him back to me when he's fully grown to take up his inheritance."

Pip was heir to their lands. Irreplaceable to the family. Mr. Roper would be furious with Eliza for helping Ruby get away. "What about you?"

"My place is here with my husband. He knows I'd never help the silly English chit my son shackled himself to. She's only ever been a burden. I've made my disapproval of you plain as day since my Liam brought you into my home."

Ruby held the woman's stare and didn't believe a word she said. Eliza wouldn't be helping her leave, giving her money, if she hadn't come to care about her welfare. Her eyes filled with tears. "All this time. You only pretended to dislike me all this time."

Eliza shrugged. "You've grown on me a little. You still babble too much, but you're a good woman, faithful to my Liam in life and in death. He'd want me to help you get back to your people."

Impulsively, Ruby hugged the woman. Eliza was stiff as a board at first, and then she suddenly embraced Ruby tightly. "You go back where you belong, lass, and find yourself a good man to marry soon. Someone who will care about the boy."

"I'll write."

Eliza pulled away. "Don't. I canna read."

Ruby blinked, shocked by that. She'd been living in this household for five years and had never once suspected Eliza was illiterate. But when she thought about it, it was always Mr.

Roper or Liam who'd read any letters that came and shared the news.

"Then I'll send something instead. Once we're settled in a good place, I'll send a warm shawl to you."

Eliza nodded. "That would be grand," she said.

Ruby stood there a moment until Eliza scowled. "Well, what are you waiting for, lass? A carriage isn't going ta come to our door to whisk you away like some fancy lady going to a ball."

"I have to wait for Pip to come back."

Eliza handed Ruby two apples and cut off some cheese, too. Then she snatched up her nearly threadbare shawl from the peg by the door. "I'll go to my husband and send Pip back to you. I didn't let him have his breakfast today, and the boy is bound to be hungry. He can eat on the journey."

She gaped at the woman who had everything arranged for her. "You planned for this."

Eliza nodded again. "Mr. Roper said he will go out to the fields, and I'll go with him to help with the lambs. You go now to your chamber and collect what you can't live without and carry upon your back. He'll be after you for the boy by sunset, so you'll have to run far and fast."

"I'll not go to my father," Ruby decided.

Eliza held up her hand. "Don't tell me what you plan. It's best I don't know so I don't have to lie about that, too. As it is, he'll likely beat me for not watching you as I should."

Ruby hugged Eliza again, afraid for the woman. "I can never thank you enough for your kindness."

"Did I ask you to? Typical Englishwoman. Always trying to fill all the peace of the world with your endless babble."

Ruby laughed, hugged Eliza one last time, and then fled for her chamber to collect the satchel already packed with her few remaining possessions from under her bed. When she got back to the kitchen, Pip was munching on the cheese left on the table and was eager to run off outside with her.

Chapter Two

LORD HECTOR STOCKWICK stuffed his book back into his satchel and looked ahead as far as he could see. Derbyshire wasn't precisely his favorite place in the winter months, but he felt a sense of anticipation as he neared the end of his journey. He had promised to meet a friend here, though he should probably refer to Lord Clement as his brother-in-law, instead. Clement had married his sister Meg ten months ago, which meant a family reunion of sorts. Hector's arrival was a surprise for Meg to make up for spending Christmas away from Cornwall for the second year in a row.

Lord Clement and most of his family—mother, brother, and sisters—had been living in Cornwall for most of the past year. Meg loved it there, but Hector had not gone back since they'd moved in. Too many memories; not all of them bad, but some he preferred never to revisit again.

He'd been rather shocked to learn that Meg had consented to spend another Christmas freezing her knees off in feet-deep snow in Derbyshire, at her husband's family's ancestral estate, The Vynes—and with Lord Vyne himself, her papa-in-law, who was not a terribly nice man. Hector trusted Lord Vyne about as far as he could throw him.

The last Hector had heard, Lord Vyne had

been in a snit over plans for his wife and unmarried children to visit Cornwall for an extended stay. Lady Vyne didn't want to return, and her son and new daughter-in-law hadn't been in any hurry to send her back to her angry husband.

But now he suspected some sort of reconciliation had taken place. Why else would Meg willingly return to a place she'd disliked so much? Meg had not hidden the fact that she'd been miserable traveling to Derbyshire last year. At least, in the beginning. Meg had fought Hector over going. She might have even hated him for dragging her from Cornwall, too. That had all changed, of course, when she'd fallen in love with Lord Clement.

Damned if Hector had seen that coming. Also, damn inconvenient to lose a fellow bachelor to the parson's noose. He couldn't even complain or tease him since the man was his brother-in-law. His sister and Clement were devilishly happy, and that was that.

Hector glanced up at the sky. It was still a few hours till total dark. The weather was holding, but he suspected it wouldn't for much longer. Thankfully, he was almost at The Vynes. He would have his feet up and a drink in hand before a cheery blaze very soon.

When the carriage topped this next rise, they began the descent into the bowl-shaped valley where the great house stood. "There it is," he said to his companion.

"Very good, sir," his new valet replied, somewhat sourly.

"Just wait, Parker," Hector promised.

"Christmas at The Vynes will be a jolly good time."

"Yes, my lord." Parker wheezed, sending steam across the carriage. "Forgive me. It's just so cold. I fear my face is frozen."

"Winter is always cold," Hector said as he regarded the poor shivering fellow. He'd been in the army or something before coming into Hector's employ. At the time of the man's interview, Hector had thought him up to the rigors of his duties in London. But he'd spoken of warm climes and even a hint of danger when he'd been taken on. Perhaps he'd no experience of winter in recent years. "I could have trained up one of the other footmen, but you were adamant you could fill my last valet's shoes."

"I'm doing my best, my lord."

"See that you do," Hector suggested as they reached the massive front door of The Vynes. Parker didn't need prodding to exit the carriage first. It was damn cold, and they both looked forward to a night of warmth and comfort before a blazing fire.

Hector got out, stretched, and then shivered as the cold wind cut through his greatcoat. "Damn, that's a bitter wind blowing." He looked at his men as they swarmed over the carriage, and then caught the coachman's eye. "There's most of a bottle of rum left inside. Dole it out to the men to warm them through when you're done taking care of the horses and carriage."

The coachman nodded, "Thank ye, sir."

He smiled quickly and made his way up

to the front door before his face froze. Belatedly, he noticed the door wasn't already opened for him, and a drift of snow had piled up before it. He yanked on the bell chain, raining ice down on himself in the process from the bell above the door, and then danced about in the cutting breeze until someone finally came.

As soon as the door opened a crack, Hector darted inside. "What took you so long?"

"I beg your pardon?" a man demanded.

Hector narrowed his eyes, not recognizing the servant. "Lord Hector Stockwick. My sister and brother-in-law are expecting me."

"And who are they?"

Hector blinked, and then looked around himself quickly, concerned for a moment that he'd barged into the wrong great house by mistake. But no. This was The Vynes. Everything was exactly as he remembered from the last time he'd been here—everything except for the servant standing before him. He must be new.

"I am here to see Lord and Lady Clement," he announced.

The man brow furrowed. "Lord and Lady Clement are not here."

"Damn, I must have beaten them and arrived first. That'll give m'sister a turn. I'm never early."

The fellow cleared his throat. "They are not expected."

"They damn well are, or I would not have come all this way in the cold for a family party."

"Who is it, Peter?" an old voice queried from the shadows.

"It's a Lord Stockwick, asking for Lord and Lady Clement," the man, Peter, replied.

Hector heard the shuffle of feet coming toward him and looked for the source. He grinned at seeing a familiar face at last—Brown, The Vynes old butler. "There you are, my good man," Hector cried.

But Hector's grin faded as he discovered a profound change in the older man's features. One side of his face was turned down at the side, and his slow progress became painful to watch.

"You've been unwell," Hector murmured, and then averted his eyes.

"Just a bit slower than I used to be, my lord," Brown murmured, pausing to draw breath. He glanced at the other servant. "Have the Green Room prepared for Lord Stockwick immediately and inform cook we've guests for dinner."

"Yes, sir." The fellow rushed off.

The old butler winced. "Forgive the confusion, my lord. Peter is new to the household and not acquainted with all the family yet."

"Ah, right. Oh, and speaking of new. This is my new valet, Parker," he announced. "I was expecting to meet my sister and Lord Clement here."

"We have not been informed of their coming, my lord, but we will now have the house prepared," he promised.

Hector glanced around, finally noticing

there were closed doors all around him, and it was almost as cold inside as out. "Who is here, sir?"

"Only Lord Vyne."

"Ah," Hector said but cringed. He and Lord Vyne were not the best of friends. Hector actually preferred it that way. "I suppose I'd better pay my respects."

"Lord Vyne will be informed of your arrival, of course, and I will have someone let you know when he might consent to see you."

"I'm in no hurry, but thank you."

The butler glanced around them; his expression was pained. "The lower rooms are not warm, my lord, so perhaps you'd like to remain in your rooms for now. I've put you in the same room you had last year. The lower rooms' fires will be lit shortly but it could take some hours for the drawing room and library to become warm enough for you."

"As long as there's a fire and bottle of port to be drunk in my room, I'll be in no hurry to come back down tonight."

"Very good, my lord," the butler said before he began another slow shuffle back to the shadows.

Hector started up the stairs immediately, Parker at his side. "Well, isn't this a cold welcome," he muttered. "I come all this way on the promise of a good time and end up nearly alone."

"Perhaps the Clements are delayed by the weather," Parker murmured soothingly. "Lord Vyne will undoubtedly be glad of your company."

"I highly doubt that," he rubbed his chilled jaw. "M'sister never quite mentioned how the old devil took his wife leaving him. He was sour before, but after that…"

"Perhaps he's mellowed."

"Not a chance," Hector warned. They reached the top of the stairs and paused to look around. "The family wing is that side, guests always to the left. Lord Vyne's chambers are the very last set of doors down there."

Those doors were closed, but a line of light shone beneath them, which Hector supposed meant the old devil was inside stewing in his juices most likely. Hector would see him soon enough, and tonight, console himself with an excellent evening of drinking alone.

He turned down the hall toward the room he'd occupied last year and found servants streaming in and out of the chamber. The bed had just finished being made up, and a maid crouched over the pitifully small fire. Parker strode in, took charge of the luggage, and then ushered the maid out, promising to take care of the fire himself. He bent low, coaxing the flames to life.

Hector threw himself on the bed, tossed a blanket over his legs and put his hands behind his head. "Good enough for now," he murmured.

A servant came to the door and cleared his throat soon after. "Lord Vyne has been informed of your arrival but is disinclined to see you this evening, my lord," the man announced

"Disinclined? Now that is a frosty

reception." He waved the servant away and caught Parker's gaze. "I told you he wouldn't have mellowed."

"I'm sorry I doubted you."

"It's quite all right. People always underestimate my wisdom." He sighed. "I suppose we ought to bunk down for the night. See what the new day brings."

"I'm sure tomorrow will be a vast deal more to your liking," Parker promised.

Hector closed his eyes, seriously considering taking a nap before dinner. "One can only hope so."

Chapter Three

HECTOR WAS SUDDENLY and rudely shaken awake. "I'm sorry to wake you, my lord, but I'll be off to find our supper."

Hector yawned, glancing around and then squinting at the dark window panes. "Is it night already?"

"A little after nine, my lord. The minute your head hit the pillow, you were asleep."

Hector scrubbed at his head. "Clement and my sister?"

"There have been no new arrivals, I'm afraid."

"Any word from Vyne?"

"Nothing."

Hector sat up. "I don't know why Vyne would be discourteous to me. I didn't have a hand in taking his wife away from him or forced his son to marry m'sister. The damn fellow couldn't be stopped from declaring that he loved Meg. What could I do? I had to agree to the match, or they might very well have eloped. If anything, it was I who have reason to be upset with *them*. I truly think she would have married him without my blessing. Imagine that."

"People in love do the strangest things," Parker agreed but he started to frown before rushing to look out the window. "There's a carriage approaching."

Hector got to his feet and stretched. "M'sister?"

"I couldn't say for sure," Parker muttered. "I don't think so. The carriage is smaller than I would expect for a traveling chaise. It is still some distance away."

"I'd better fortify myself with a stiff drink before I go back downstairs."

Parker left the window and started to pour Hector's drink.

"Give it over," Hector said as he drew near. He took a warming swallow and smiled. "Only the best at The Vynes," he murmured to himself. "I have missed that this past year."

Parker returned to the window, and Hector joined him in looking out. There was indeed a carriage drawing closer. He could see a pair of lamps swinging back and forth, carried by men guiding the horses down the long drive. But with so little illumination, there wasn't much else he could make out.

While Parker straightened the bed, Hector continued to track the carriage's progress, warming himself with another small glass of Lord Vyne's excellent port. The carriage reached the house finally, but then circled to the servants' entrance. "Not m'sister."

Hector moved to the far window, threw aside the drape in a bid to see more below.

A cloaked figure clambered out, and then reached back inside the carriage. Hector was taken aback to see a child jump into those outstretched arms. Instinct told him the cloaked figure was female. "A lady and child," he mused out loud.

"What was that?"

"I said the carriage just brought a woman and child to the servants' entrance."

Parker came to see, too. "Odd."

Hector followed their progress until he couldn't see them anymore. But he was sure they had come in. "How is it odd?"

"I don't know, but…"

"I'm curious too," he murmured. His stomach rumbled. "Be a good fellow and go below and bring me back my supper. While you're there, find out what's afoot."

"Yes, sir," Parker promised before slipping from the room.

Hector glanced out the window again, noting the carriage was being turned around to leave again. "Now, who would visit Lord Vyne with a young child on a night like this?"

Intrigued, he headed for the door and stepped outside into the hall to take a peek, only to dart back inside his room when he saw movement. Three figures were just down the hall at the top of the staircase.

Hector peeked out carefully again, noticing they were moving toward the family wing. No. Not just the family wing…but directly to Lord Vyne's bedchamber door.

The distant door opened, and for a brief moment, the trio was illuminated. A woman and child's outlines were as clear as day beside Peter, the butler's stand-in. They entered, but Peter remained outside. And then the bedchamber door shut behind the new arrivals, throwing the hall into darkness again.

Hector withdrew into his room as Peter

headed for the stairs and rushed down them loudly.

When all was quiet, Hector risked another peek. The hall was empty now. Eerily still.

Hector took a few steps toward the family wing, feeling an odd sense of concern about the woman and child arriving so late at night. It smacked of a scandal in the making. If that were true, he'd better find out the details before Clement and Meg came.

"My lord, is something the matter?" Parker queried from directly behind Hector.

Hector spun about, caught by surprise. He was about to complain about Parker's stealth when he noticed a footman standing behind his new valet. "No. Just stretching my legs."

The footman stepped forward, his expression grim as he held a large tray. "Your supper, my lord."

"Yes, good." He cast a discreet glance toward Lord Vyne's chambers and then headed back into his warmer room, where the tray was being set on a low table before a chair nearest the fire.

Hector picked at the food until the footman was gone. "That woman and child were taken into Lord Vyne's private chambers. What did you learn below?"

Parker whistled. "Perhaps that's the cause?"

"Of what?"

"The odd feeling I just got from the other servants. I know I'm a stranger, but the mood below stairs is grim. No one is talking, and I sense the servants in the kitchen couldn't wait for me to leave again." Parker's lips twitched.

"But perhaps it's nothing at all, and I imagined the strangeness where none exists."

The man had good instincts. "Get back down there."

"Why?"

Although he didn't have to explain himself to his valet, he wanted to impress upon Parker a sense of urgency. "My sister is due to arrive, and her delicate state…"

Parker nodded. "You don't want her made upset if there's a scandal brewing. I understand."

Hector nodded. "Find out who that woman is before morning comes, and I'll double your wages."

"Yes, sir," Parker agreed, eyes alight with a mix of greed and excitement.

Chapter Four

RUBY ROPER HUGGED her son tightly to her chest. The little boy was sleeping soundly in her arms at last. Their journey had been hard for him. The cold and urgency of their flight from Scotland had unsettled him. Surely it couldn't be too much longer before they met her uncle, Lord Vyne, and they could finally rest.

If they were to receive the help they needed from Lord Vyne, and perhaps be allowed to stay at one of the family estates, they had to make a good impression. She had hoped to see her aunt and cousins, too, but they hadn't come yet. Ruby was sure that with their support, the matter of her son's future would be easily achieved.

Ruby had only the vaguest idea of where she was in the Vynes' mansion. Her last visit was years ago, long before her marriage. Tonight she'd been brought through dark corridors to this small reception room with no conversation other than she was to follow and wait.

Ruby adjusted her son in her lap, striving to ease the discomfort of sitting in the same position for an hour. At least they were warm at last. A cheerful fire burned in the hearth below the clock, and plenty of fuel had been added to it to ensure their comfort.

The servant appeared again, a pitcher in hand, and disappeared into the other room without looking her way.

A few minutes later, the servant returned and cleared his throat. "Lord Vyne will see you now, Mrs. Roper."

"Thank you."

Ruby shook her boy until Pip stirred. Sleepy gray eyes blinked open. "Mama?"

"Shh, my darling. We're to see Lord Vyne now. Remember what we practiced on the journey."

Pip nodded quickly and wriggled to be set down. Pip smoothed his hands down his rough waistcoat and then tugged on his too-short sleeves. As with any small boy, he usually cared little for his appearance. He tossed his head, removing his sandy hair from his eyes and nodded that he was ready.

Ruby smiled down on him. Poor Pip had been through so much since their flight from Scotland. She had uprooted him from everything he'd ever known. He missed his home, and his granny, too. She took hold of his tiny hand and they moved toward the servant side by side.

The man gestured her toward the open doorway.

Ruby glimpsed shadows beyond and not much else. But she moved into the room, tugging her son with her because she had no choice.

The room was a bedchamber, and her uncle sat before the fire in a chair, one booted foot carelessly thrown over the other. He did not rise upon seeing her but beckoned her close impatiently.

"It's a pleasure to see you again, Uncle," she murmured as she dipped a deep curtsy. Beside her, Pip bowed. "May I introduce my son, Pip, to you?"

"I never expected to see you again, Niece," Uncle said in a disapproving tone. "I thought you were gone from us forever."

Although startled by his tone, Ruby kept her chin up. She was not ashamed of her actions. She'd married for love. "My husband died last year, sir. I missed home and my family."

His eyes narrowed. "Your father's home is still some miles away, girl. Much farther south."

"I could not pass The Vynes estate without paying my respects to you first."

He grunted. "Well, then, don't just stand there, girl. Come closer so I may see you better by the fire's light."

Ruby quickly complied and bore a long stare that took in her appearance from head to toe without flinching. She was very conscious that her gown was years old and desperately needed replacement, her cuffs worn. His gaze then flickered to her son Pip and lingered, before he gazed into the flames again.

"You look like your mother," Lord Vyne remarked.

"I think so too," Ruby murmured, looking down at Pip with a fond smile.

"I was speaking of you, Mrs. Roper. Your mother was a beauty in her youth. Quite the catch for my brother, then. She may not have had much of a dowry, but men were lining up just to speak with her." His expression soured, and he looked up at Ruby again. "Your ill-advised marriage ruined your chances of reaching your fullest potential."

Ruby trembled a little. "I have never regretted the choices I made, Uncle."

Vyne snorted. "As difficult as your mother was, too, I see, which explains why you'd willingly run off to marry a poor farmer's son."

"He was a good man, kind to me. A good father to Pip." She'd known her marriage would make her unpopular within the family, but she'd expected at least cordial civility from her uncle. "I see I shouldn't have come."

Vyne shook his head. "Sit down."

She did, and Pip, to his credit, neatly lowered himself to the seat beside her instead of dropping like a stone as had always been his custom.

In the light of the fire, she got a better look at her uncle. He seemed to have changed very much. There was a lot more gray in his hair than she remembered, and the lines on his face were deeper. She didn't wonder about the lack of a smile for her. He'd never smiled at her before that she could remember. "I am glad to find you in good health, Uncle."

One of his brows rose. "Is that so?"

"Yes, of course. Why, you've hardly changed at all since I was last here as a girl," she promised.

His eyes narrowed. "There's no need to butter me up."

"I wasn't speaking untruths," she promised but then began to feel uncomfortable.

Uncle began to tap on the arm of his chair. "What is it you want with me, Niece? And I do know you want something."

She dropped her gaze a little. "My husband's sudden passing revealed how unwanted I was in his family. They had intended to bind me in marriage to a man I'd never met."

"You should be grateful they considered your future at all by arranging a marriage," Uncle Vyne suggested.

"I was not consulted until it was nearly too late to avoid the connection. I believe the marriage would have brought further disgrace upon me." She lifted her gaze to her uncle. "I feel sure my family would not have approved of me marrying a potato farmer. He was not wealthy or important. He was not a suitable connection."

"That describes your unfortunate marriage, too."

"I was young and in love. But I am older now and ready to make amends."

Vyne narrowed his eyes. "You fled from them, just as you did from your father's home."

She wet her lips. "I had no choice. Mr. Roper has not allowed me to write to any member of my family since my husband's death. I wanted to ask your advice."

Vyne started nodding again. "You did the right thing coming here first. Your father washed his hands of you long ago."

Ruby winced.

"And he would not wish you to return home to spoil your younger sisters' chance of making a good match by stirring up that old scandal you made again."

She had worried about them, too. "What should I do then? I need to provide for my son. Pip needs a home and a gentleman's education befitting a member of our family. Will you help us?"

"At least you possess the wit to come to me. You are your father's daughter, all right, but at least you're honest about why you want my support," Lord Vyne grumbled. "Alexander always had his hand out."

Ruby knew that. Father supported his family as well as he did because of the grudging generosity of his elder brother. For herself, she needed very little. "I hoped you might take an interest in my son's future."

Uncle pursed his lips as he studied them both for several uncomfortable minutes. His expression was inscrutable. Ruby glanced at her son, who'd remained silent at her side, and she saw that he was drowsing off to sleep. She quickly nudged him until he opened his eyes wide again.

"How old is the boy?" Uncle asked at last.

"Pip is four years and five months old."

"Healthy? Strong?"

"Yes. Pip is very smart, too. I have already begun teaching him his letters, and he is a very keen student of mathematics and geography."

Uncle waved her remarks away. "I will consider later what I might do for him. As for you…"

Ruby held her breath.

He squinted even more. "I will require something in return for any assistance. I will expect you to marry a man of my choosing to wipe away the disgrace you brought upon the family," he warned her. "I will have the final say, young lady. I will brook no argument, or you may leave tonight."

Ruby had been expecting such a requirement, but from her father, not her uncle. She did need protection, and a biddable husband would certainly help her cause, too. It was not the way she'd want to make a second marriage, but Ruby was prepared to say yes to any good man recommended to her, if it meant food in her son's belly.

She inclined her head. "I would be pleased to meet any gentleman you and my aunt might suggest, Uncle."

"I expect you to comport yourself as a lady while you are here, Mrs. Roper," Uncle said suddenly. "You will not speak of your unfortunate marriage to anyone after today without expressing the deepest regret for your past actions."

"As you wish, my lord," Ruby agreed, but her cheeks burned. Ruby would never regret her marriage to Liam. "I promise I will give you no trouble, Uncle, but might I speak of my husband with my aunt?"

"No, you may not," he snapped. "Keep your son out of sight for the time being, too. Now, off with you before I change my mind."

Ruby fled for the door, dragging Pip along in her wake.

Chapter Five

HECTOR COULD HAVE SPENT this Christmas in London, gambling, drinking, and whoring with his closest friends. Instead, he was sitting before a massive marble fireplace, feeling the warmth caress his cheeks in frozen Derbyshire. Hector wore a pair of new wool breeches, his best Wellington boots, and had rested his feet upon a tasseled velvet stool. But there was no one to see his sartorial splendor—he was utterly alone and quietly miserable in his solitude.

He glanced around the cavernous library with weary resignation. He doubted half the titles up there had been read in years, but they certainly looked impressive. That was the sad story of The Vynes. It might impress at first glance, but when you looked beneath, spent any length of time here, you soon found out that was as far as the thrill ever went.

Lord Vyne rarely came downstairs, or so he'd been told over his lonely breakfast. So upon hearing that, Hector had toured the downstairs rooms and elected to make himself at home in this chamber until Meg and Clement arrived. Less work for the servants. Less disturbance for him. He had everything he needed within easy reach.

Across the room, there was an exceptional array of spirits to consume later. Hector would eat his luncheon upon Lord Vyne's huge and unused mahogany desk and put his feet up on it afterward. No one would know because no one was here. But he expected that by afternoon, he'd be ensconced in one of the four deep-padded window seats, which provided outstanding views the estate, even in inclement weather. Or perhaps he'd take a nap.

A storm raged outside just now, and there wasn't a chance in hell he'd bother to stir himself to go and look about the district or visit the local tavern. A pity. There had been a charming piece of fancy at the distant inn he'd enjoyed upon his visit last year. He'd planned to see her again, and might even now have been entangled with her but for the foul weather.

But Meg had still not yet arrived, so he was stuck waiting for her to come. Once he'd spoken a few words with his sister and brother-in-law, dined with them once or twice, he'd probably slip away discreetly and avoid those disapproving scenes Meg was so fond of creating in recent years when he drank too much.

But in this weather, until Meg arrived, Hector would be better off amusing himself right here in this warm, well-appointed chamber.

"Here is your journal, my lord."

Hector was startled by the abruptness of hearing his valet's voice ringing out right behind him, and yelped. "Would you please learn to scuff your boot as you enter a room, Parker. If I were advanced in years and possessed of a weak heart, you'd have me finished off, and you'd be seeking new employment," he complained even as he held out his hand for the journal.

"Apologies, my lord," Parker murmured as a slight weight settled on Hector's palm.

He brought the journal to his chest and caressed the familiar leather. "What news?"

"No one is talking still. Not about her or the child."

"Is she still here?"

"Indeed, yes. A large breakfast tray was sent to her chamber early."

"One to the nursery, too?"

"No. The nursery remains empty."

Wealthy women did not often share their beds, their chambers, with their offspring. They shunted them off to the servants to care for their needs. Lord Clement had been assigned four servants by his father when he was a boy, and Hector, from a slightly less-well-off family, had been granted two. "What about her servants?"

"There are plenty about, but none of them seem to belong to the lady. I was curious about the child and went up to see for myself. The nursery is empty and quite cold. Nothing is being done to make it ready for habitation yet."

"Perhaps the child has gone."

"No one has left the estate since the carriage departed last night, my lord. Not in this weather." He shrugged. "There is a visitor expected in a few days, though."

"Who is it?"

"No one would say."

"Ah, well that's something to look forward to." Hopefully not another of Vyne's unwelcome surprises like last year. Last year, Vyne had tried to match his son with the daughter of one of his toadies. "Keep your ears open."

"Yes, my lord."

Hector hoped that whoever was coming was someone nearer to his age rather than Lord Vyne's. Older men tended to become stodgy and humorless. Lord Vyne was a prime example of what happened when men reached a certain age.

He peered at his valet, who was still hovering at his side. "Any word from Lord Vyne?"

"None, my lord. I believe he does not rise early, though."

"Or at all. Well, perhaps I'll see Vyne in the afternoon." But for now, it seemed the morning was likely free to spend as he liked. He couldn't imagine Clement forging on in this dreadful weather, not with Meg along and likely complaining of the cold every half-mile. "You can go. Why don't you go butter up a maid and find out more about our mysterious lady guest?"

The fellow's eyes lit up with amusement. "Shall I take that as an order to consort, my lord?"

He shrugged. "As close as you'll ever get from me, I should think. But remember, I'll not rescue you from any below-stairs scandal should you get a child on any chit. You'd have to marry her etcetera, etcetera."

"Never fear. Like you, I value my independence far too much to make such a careless mistake with a woman." He bowed and sauntered from the room, leaving Hector to his solitary comforts.

But first.

The journal.

Hector got to his feet, rounded the impressive library desk, and sat down in the well-padded leather chair. He reached for quill and ink and added a few words about his arrival at The Vynes. There wasn't very much to say, unfortunately.

December 18 ~ Dreadful weather. Arrived before Meg and Clement. Lord Vyne indisposed to conversation. Port before bedtime an excellent vintage. Slept well. Breakfast ham was a little dry. Mysterious guests intrigue me.

Chore done, Hector closed the book. He'd kept a daily record of his life from the moment he'd inherited the title. In those pages were scandals and conquests, joy and heartbreak. All the things he'd experienced. He did not censor himself. He wrote the unvarnished truth so that his own son would know more of him than Hector had of his father.

He was about to rise from the desk when a child suddenly raced into the room—a small boy, wearing a rumpled brown suit. The child's face was narrow and pointed, hair pale and falling to his shoulders. The child laughed before flopping onto a wide velvet chaise.

A willowy beauty raced into the room,

scolding someone called Pip about daring to run away. They did not see Hector sitting across the chamber, so they carried on with their own business.

The woman punched her hands to her hips but smiled down at the boy. "What am I going to do with you, young man?"

"Love me," the boy replied, giggling as he wriggled on his back on the velvet chaise looking up at her.

"Oh, I do love you, my lad," the woman said as she scooped up the child and hugged him tightly. "More than you'll ever know. Forever and ever and ever."

It was a sweet scene, but it was a private moment he shouldn't have witnessed. He ought to announce himself before they burst into songs about love and other such nonsense.

Hector stood and cleared his throat.

But he wasn't quite prepared for the impact of the mother's beauty when she turned to face him. The woman was stunningly pretty with wavy dark hair and wide blue eyes. Her full red lips parted in surprise; her delicate, ring-less left hand rose to the base of her throat. He feared for a moment that she might scream. But instead, she quickly curtsied and apologized.

The boy bowed, too, quite flawlessly for someone so young.

Hector approached them slowly, drawn in by the pair and the chance for conversation. The lady was a fetching wench indeed, one he felt keen to become acquainted with. Perhaps

Hector might just get his Christmas wish for an enjoyable holiday after all.

Hector extended one leg and swept into a deep bow worthy of a court appointment. Women tended to enjoy being treated like queens in their own right. "Forgive the start my presence must have caused you. You must be another of Lord Vyne's Christmas house guests."

The woman nodded. "How do you do?"

"Very well, and all the better for seeing you and your son." Hector glanced around, but there was no one to introduce them. He wouldn't let that dissuade him from talking to her, though. "I had started to feel I might be the only soul about the house, save for the servants."

She looked toward the boy for a moment. "My son has an energetic disposition and is still of an age to think it funny to elude me. Forgive us the disturbance."

"No apologies are necessary." Hector looked at the child now, feeling he should acknowledge the boy if he wanted to make the best impression with the mother. He extended his hand. "How do you do? Pip, isn't it?"

The boy nodded.

"You shouldn't run away from your pretty mama like that. You could be easily lost in a house this size, and she might never find you. Make sure you stay close to her from now on."

The boy hugged his mama's skirts. "I won't be lost."

The woman hugged her son to her side. "Forgive me, but who are you?"

He didn't mind that the woman made a bold request to find out his identity. She'd saved him the trouble of dropping his name and title into the conversation. "Lord Stockwick, madam."

"I see," she said, then her eyes narrowed. "Stockwick, did you say?"

"Indeed. I see you are familiar with the family name."

"I was, once, but I've been away a long time. I remember an older man—with gray whiskers—held the title then."

"Ah, you must be thinking of my father, whom I am happy to say I don't at all resemble. There's no gray in my whiskers, as you see. Were you very well acquainted with him?"

"Only in passing. I recall a daughter, though I am afraid it has been many years since I've thought of her. I cannot remember her name."

"Margaret. Or perhaps you knew her as Meg."

"Oh, yes. That's it. Meg. We spent some time together right here. Well, upstairs in the nursery."

"Then *we* are likely already acquainted, too."

"I don't recall meeting someone like you," she began, her frown growing as she peered at him. "Unless…"

"Hector," he supplied, and then smiled as she appeared to recognize his name.

But her eyes had narrowed upon him.

"Oh, it's *you*. I don't suppose you're here to return the silver bell you stole from me."

"I…" He gaped, stunned. "Ruby Clement?"

"Ruby Roper. Mrs. Ruby Roper." She scowled. "So will you at last admit the truth?"

"I…" he began, but then her request sank in. "I admit you accused me of theft of that ridiculous thing when we were children."

"It was not ridiculous," she argued, voice rising. "That bell meant a great deal to me."

Hector punched his hands on his hips. "Well, I didn't take it."

"Do you swear?" she asked.

"Every day and every way I can," he shot back. "I was falsely accused, and you owe me an apology."

For a moment, Ruby seemed taken aback by his statement, but then her face pinked with a blush, and she looked down. Her child had moved between them, looking up at them with a bewildered expression.

Hector took a pace back, appalled by his heated outburst. He hadn't seen Ruby in a dozen years, and she could still stir up his temper over something so inconsequential as a silver bell. The way she'd done as a girl, too. He remembered they had become bitter enemies over the lost bell, but those childish fits of rage belonged in his past.

Ruby Clement had lost a silver bell somewhere in this vast pile, and Hector had the unfortunate luck to be the last person to admit that he had seen it. And because he had, he'd been suspected—by Ruby, mostly. His possessions had been searched, and he'd even been deprived of a meal in a bid to entice him to admit the bell's location. He should have kept his mouth shut instead of trying to help with the search. He'd never coveted the stupid bell, since he had one of his own.

"Forgive me," he murmured. "I should not have raised my voice to you."

"No, I beg you to forgive *me*, my lord. Apparently, some losses never lie quietly in the mind. I hadn't truly thought of my bell in years."

"Well, no harm done." He took pains to calm his ruffled feathers. He was no longer a little boy who needed everyone to believe he spoke the truth. He swept his hair back from his eyes, noting his brow was damp and hot. "Well, that little disagreement between us certainly got the blood pumping through my veins on a day I thought would be utterly uneventful. No chance of being chilled for a while now, eh, Mrs. Roper? Would you care to sit down with me so we might conduct a more civilized conversation and renew our acquaintance? It has been some time since we last met. I'm sure much has happened since that we could catch up about. I must admit, I haven't kept up with news from that side of Lord Vyne's family."

She shook her head and turned away. "I really should return Pip upstairs. Excuse me."

Hector was keen not to let her go away yet. He had been rather bored until she'd swept into the room, and the chance to talk to a near-stranger was vastly more appealing than watching the snowfall outside. "If you're worrying about Lord Vyne's restriction denying the chance for children to be in the lower part of the mansion, I happen to have it on good authority that he rarely comes downstairs these days."

She stopped and turned. "Why ever not?"

"He hardly ever comes down." Hector drew closer so he could whisper.

"Oh!" she gasped. "But still, Lady Vyne might not want Pip running around."

He looked at her in confusion. "Surely you've heard? Lady Vyne is not here. She left Vyne almost a year ago. Took the children, packed her trunks, and has been living in Cornwall with Lord Clement and m'sister Meg —whom he married by the way."

"He never told me about my aunt."

Hector rolled his eyes. "Vyne lies, quite frequently, and he is known for keeping his own counsel, especially when it's a sensitive topic. I really would not put much faith in anything he might promise, too, if I were you."

She pulled her child to her side and stroked his pale hair. "I'm sure that's not the case. He wouldn't lie to me. I'm his niece. Family."

"Then you might be a rare bird indeed, but I am not wrong about your aunt." Hector gestured her to the arrangement of chairs before the warm fire. "Please join me."

Ruby shook her head again. "Do excuse us."

To his regret, Ruby flew from the room, dragging her son along with her. Hector followed along a few steps, but she was soon only a memory.

A pity she went so quickly. He'd only now remembered that Ruby Clement was the first girl he'd ever kissed. Since it was Christmas, and she was quite pretty, he hoped to be in a position to claim a second under the mistletoe…and do a much better job this year.

Chapter Six

RUBY RETURNED her son to her chamber, told him to play quietly, and then went in search of a servant. Hector suggested she had been lied to, but that couldn't be right. Her uncle surely would have told her of her aunt's absence when she asked to talk of her marriage with the woman. And she'd experienced enough of Hector as a boy not to believe anything he would say without confirming it first.

At last she found a maid, who stammered out that Lady Vyne was not receiving.

That didn't sound promising. "Perhaps you could ask if Lady Vyne would make an exception for her eldest niece."

"It's not my place to interrupt her, madam," the girl warned.

Ruby narrowed her eyes, suspecting she was being lied to again. "Then whose is it?"

The maid wet her lips and became visibly distressed. "I could ask the housekeeper."

Ruby could ask, too, and get the answer she wanted in quicker time. "I should like to speak to the housekeeper myself."

The maid's eyes grew round.

"Take me to her," she said. "Now."

The little maid uttered a muffled wail.

Ruby hadn't been so long in the wilderness of Scotland not to remember how to deal with reluctant servants. "I hope you're not going to tell me the housekeeper is too busy to speak with a member of Lord Vyne's family," Ruby asked, raising one brow.

"No, madam," the maid promised as she bobbed a curtsy and bid her follow her to the main staircase.

They went down to the entrance hall together but turned away from the sealed front doors and the library, where Lord Stockwick might still be if she bothered to look. Behind the stairs, there was an entrance to the servants' hall below. Although, at first glance, it seemed merely a paneled wall rather than a doorway.

Ruby descended after the maid, skirts lifted to clear the steps. The passage down was narrow, and the air musty and cold, and Ruby was very happy to see light seeping around a lower door.

They burst out into the warm, fragrant air of the servants' hall. The scent of roasting meat and baking bread was strong and reminded her of her former Scotland home. Farther down the hall, she could see servants bent over a large worktable, consulting each other as they toiled for Lord Vyne.

"This way, madam," the maid urged in a whisper.

Ruby was turned away from the kitchen staff and shown to a plain oak door with a brass plaque attached to it. *Housekeeper.*

The maid knocked and entered when bid.

Ruby waited outside a moment to give the maid a chance to explain her presence, and then stepped into the room. A severe-looking woman with gray hair and dark clothes sat behind a small desk sipping tea, but set that aside quickly when she spotted Ruby.

Ruby smiled. "You must be the housekeeper."

"Yes, I am Mrs. Burrows. I am housekeeper of The Vynes."

Ruby didn't remember meeting the woman on her last visit. "I am hoping you can help me speak with Lady Vyne today."

Mrs. Burrows pursed her lips, and then she sent the maid away. "She is not to be disturbed. Is there something I can help you with?"

"Yes, the truth would be appreciated. Is my aunt here or not?"

Again the woman pursed her lips. "I shall be happy to pass a message to Lord Vyne that you wish to speak with the countess."

"If I wanted to trouble my uncle, I would have already asked him about his wife a second time," she said quietly.

The housekeeper's jaw twitched. "You will have to wait to speak with Lord Vyne."

"Why will you not tell me about my aunt's whereabouts? I promise you, I hold her in the highest esteem. Is she in ill health?"

"Not that I'm aware of."

"A housekeeper would know everything there is to know about the occupants of the house she is mistress of," Ruby argued. "I can only conclude that my aunt is not here, and I also suspect now that my uncle doesn't want her location divulged by the servants. Not even to me."

The housekeeper tilted her head to one side. "I cannot help what you suspect."

"No, you cannot." Ruby pulled a face. Hector had told the truth about Lord Vyne's marriage. "How sad that I will likely not see her. There was so much I hoped to ask her."

"I am sorry I could not be more help."

Ruby nodded slowly. "Thank you for seeing me. But one last question. I don't suppose you ever found the silver bell I lost when I was here last time."

"I am sorry to say it is not in my possession, madam, or I would have gladly returned it to you long ago," the housekeeper promised as she led Ruby back into the hallway door.

If her bell was not in the housekeeper's possession, or her servants, it meant it had been well and truly lost all those years ago. Seeing Hector again here had stirred up an irrational hope she might be reunited with her long-lost keepsake, but it was not to be.

As she was about to ask another question, the housekeeper spoke again. "Should you require anything within our power, the servants of The Vynes are at your disposal. Please use the bells of the house next time."

In other words, no more browbeating the servants into bringing her downstairs again. It wasn't a surprising request. By rights, Ruby ought to have kept to the upper floors where the family normally would spend all of their time. "Perhaps next time I have a question, the maids might simply do me the courtesy of telling me what I need to know."

The housekeeper inclined her head.

The maid was waiting beside the servants' stairs and led her back up to the entrance hall without another word. They parted ways upstairs, not far from Ruby's chamber.

If her aunt was not here, and her cousins were not here, but on their way, she was in for a cold and lonely Christmas indeed, worrying over who her uncle might want her to marry in exchange for his help.

"You only had to look in this room to learn I was telling the truth," Lord Stockwick said suddenly, startling her out of her wits. He was standing just down the hall, his hand on a door latch. He pushed the door wide and stepped back with a smile. "The countess' chamber is right here, just down from yours."

Ruby wet her lips and hurried forward, sweeping past him to see for herself. She entered a room covered in white cloths and so cold, she shivered.

"They're all like that. Cold and closed up," Lord Stockwick promised.

Ruby didn't remember this chamber.

Hector went to a wall and tugged on a white cloth draped over a picture frame, showering himself in the dust. He uncovered a portrait of her aunt as Ruby remembered her looking years go.

Hector cursed softly, batting at his sleeves and dusty hair. "I should have known that would happen," he complained, and then he sneezed. "She hasn't lived in this room for ten months or more."

"The servants have been neglectful."

"The servants were probably ordered to shut up the room and forget the countess even existed." Hector shook his head. "He's a spiteful, nasty man, your uncle. You'd best be cautious of him and whatever plans he has for you."

"Why do you think he has plans for me?"

"I have been Clement's confidant for many years. Vyne makes plans for everyone in his family and cares little what you all think of them, so long as he has his way."

Distressed by that remark, Ruby went to the window and drew back the drape to look out. This room was at the front of the house, overlooking the drive. The best view, she thought. Lord Vyne's bedchamber was on the other side of the house in a similar position of importance. "What do you suspect he is planning for me?"

"I don't know, which makes me suspicious. Last year he made a wager with his son. Dangling freedom for Lady Vyne and her children if he wed within three months. He'd even gone so far as to pick out the bride, too."

"But didn't you say Clement married your sister?"

"A mistake in the wording of the wager that I don't think he'll make again. Clement married my sister because he fell in love with her, winning the wager true—but not how Lord Vyne intended things to turn out." Hector scrubbed his jaw. "You said you were Mrs. Roper now?"

Ruby always hated when people

questioned her marital status. "Yes. I'm a widow," she admitted.

"Ah, then you ought to be careful you don't find yourself married again too quickly," he warned. "Vyne is not above using his own family to settle his debts with an advantageous match that profits him more than you."

"I'm sure he wouldn't do that to me," she lied, knowing full well she *had* put her future in her uncle's control.

Hector shrugged. "Suit yourself, but don't say I didn't warn you when the next arrival at The Vynes turns out to be a bachelor in want of a wife."

She looked at him curiously. "Are you married?"

His eyes narrowed. "No, and I intend to stay this way for a long time to come," he promised before excusing himself and sauntering back out into the hall.

Chapter Seven

HECTOR WAS RUDELY AWAKENED by the clang of a fire poker striking the hearth. "Do you have to do that now?"

"Sorry, my lord," Parker apologized. "The fire needs to be relit."

Hector pulled himself up from his warm bed and scowled at his valet. "Why did you let it go out in the first place?"

"It won't happen again. I've been trying to find out more about Mrs. Roper for you and the guest who is expected to arrive. It has been a frustrating morning all round. The servants here are less forthcoming than any I've ever met."

"Vyne's influence, I'm sure," Hector concluded.

He shivered. The room was damn cold, and Hector only wore the bedsheet and a thick blanket over him. He never wore a nightshirt, preferring nothing to come between him and the perfect night of rest. Uncomfortably chilled, he glanced over the side of the bed, but his clothes from last night were missing from the floor. Cursing his new valet's efficiency, Hector burrowed back under the bedding. His last man had known not to do any valeting before luncheon.

But it was no use. Hector was cold and wide awake. He'd have to get up and dress.

Bracing himself, he rolled out of bed and rushed to his traveling trunks, pawing through his clothes to find his warmest garments urgently.

"My lord, please, don't ruin my morning's work on your wardrobe," Parker cried out in anguish. "I had everything pressed and ready to wear."

"I want my warmest clothes on me today." Hector spared the discarded clothing a fleeting glance. "I'd like not to freeze to death."

"Here, let me help you," the man offered, easing between him and the remaining clothing. He offered up an undershirt, then a recently ironed white linen shirt. Hose came next, then long trousers that secured under the arch of his foot. He put on his favorite boots and the thickest wool waistcoat he owned, and then a brown wool coat, longer than he'd typically wear. Hector had come to The Vynes prepared for the great chill of the place.

Finally starting to warm up, he moved to the fire but quickly saw the pitiful flames would never warm him the rest of the way. "You cannot allow the fire to die down again. This is the coldest place on earth. There must always be a good fire in my room. Always."

"I'm sorry, my lord," Parker said as he rushed to the fire again and began to poke it.

The fire, if anything, burned a little less. This would never do. "Stop poking it. Give it time to catch properly again."

Parker finally sat back on his heels and rubbed his arms. "This might take a while."

"Yes, it probably will."

Parker looked up at him "I believe there is a good fire burning just down the hall in the upstairs parlor."

"That will have to do." He frowned. "Why was the upstairs parlor lit?"

"Mrs. Roper and her son are there already," Parker explained, adding a little kindling to the meager flames.

"Ah," Hector murmured. "The widow."

Parker looked up at him again. "Is there something wrong?"

"Yes. No. She's a widow," he complained.

"Why is that an issue? Were you not a frequent companion of Lady Freemont's, a widow, just last month?"

"The month before." Hector scowled. "You know, for a relatively new employee, you know far too much about my life."

"I can't help it if *your* servants talk, my lord," he murmured, adding more fuel to the fire before standing up to face him. "It is a regrettable facet of downstairs life in every place but here."

Hector grunted. "The problem is she, Mrs. Roper, is Lord Vyne's niece, and…"

"And?"

"I find her much too attractive."

"Pretty women are one of life's joys," Parker suggested with a cheeky smile.

"Indeed they are quite the distraction. Except when there is a genuine danger of becoming leg-shackled to one by accident."

"Is that likely here?"

Hector sighed. "Normally when confronted by a pretty woman, I wouldn't hesitate to spend time with them. Alone, preferably. The boy is a deterrent to a romantic pursuit, surely, but I find myself wondering about her, and that isn't good. Perhaps it is the solitude of the place that draws me to her. But here, at this time, the lady has no chaperone but the boy, no family but Lord Vyne, and he is keeping to his chambers. If my sister were here, I'd have reason to linger in her presence to learn more about her, and perhaps who knows where that could lead. But I would not appreciate compromising Mrs. Roper by mistake because of a lack of chaperone."

"I see your point. Being forced to marry would be unpleasant."

Hector grunted.

"However, can you ignore Mrs. Roper until Lord and Lady Clement arrive? That seems a touch rude when there's little here to amuse either one of you."

Parker was only repeating what Hector himself had thought about last night, as he'd bid her good night. He couldn't avoid her too much and not be considered rude. "I agree."

"Well, you'll just have to be discreet about how much time you spend together. Lord Vyne has not left his room in several days, and it is freezing today."

"So you suspect he might not come out at all."

Parker nodded. "I could keep watch for Lord Vyne or his man, and warn you if anyone starts lurking if you like."

"That won't be necessary," Hector warned. "I am quite capable of discretion."

"Suit yourself. But I have to admit that if I were in your shoes, I probably wouldn't regret having to marry someone like Mrs. Roper under any circumstances. She is very lovely to look at."

Hector studied the man sourly. "Keep your eyes on the fire."

"Yes, my lord." Parker chuckled softly. "I'd suggest you hurry along to that warm room before you catch a chill."

Hector glanced behind Parker and saw the flames had died out entirely while they'd been conversing. "Yes, I suppose I should go. You've somehow managed to put the fire out completely now."

Parker uttered a curse and then knelt before the hearth to tend the fire again.

Hector left him to it, found gloves and his scarf, and wrapped the latter around his neck for the short journey down the hall. But he found himself rather too keen to be given any excuse to spend time with the delectable Mrs. Roper. She *was* rather lovely and, if not for the boy, available.

Chapter Eight

A TAP at the door woke Ruby from a fitful doze. "Come in?" she called, even as she checked to see what her son was up to. Pip seemed happy with his collection of old toys, but his eyes lit up as Lord Stockwick entered the room.

"Forgive my intrusion, but might I join you? My valet is having a devilishly hard time keeping my fire going in my chamber."

"Of course, you can," she promised, rushing to smooth out her skirts. "Please come in and warm yourself by the fire."

He shut the door behind him and rushed to the fireside, holding his hands to the flames. "Another cheerful, warm day at The Vynes," he complained sarcastically.

"Yes, it is miserable weather we are having." Ruby smiled. "I had hoped to take Pip out, but I'm afraid we'd get lost or buried up to our necks in a drift before we'd gone twenty steps into the gardens."

Stockwick glanced her way and smiled, too. "You'd be all right if you kept to the known paths."

She laughed. "I haven't any idea where they might be, or even go under all that snow."

"I'd find you," he promised. "But you really should visit again in the summer. The paths are quite extensive. You can go all the way up to the highest ridge. The views take your breath away."

"You like it here?" she asked, realizing he spoke so fondly of the place.

He shrugged. "I suppose I do. And I'm not one for rusticating."

"High praise indeed then." She watched him warm himself by the fire for a while. She'd been hoping she would meet him again today. She found herself almost as restless as her son. And curious about the boy she'd once known and bickered with. She wanted to know if he really had changed--beyond the improvement of his looks. He was much more handsome now than when he'd been a boy. Talking with him also gave her the chance to learn more about society and the common view of world events from a different angle. "Where is your estate located?"

"I don't have one. I live in London year-round."

"I thought all titles came with entailed property."

"Not in my case, which was something of a relief. I never liked the estate my father lived in."

"Too many bad memories?"

"Not enough good ones," Hector told her, and then came to sit in a nearby chair. "But I want to hear about you, Mrs. Roper. Where has life taken you in recent years?"

Uncle Vyne had suggested she keep her history to herself, but hiding her marriage went against the grain. "To Scotland, a little village over the border."

He nodded. "I thought I detected a trace of an accent."

She put her fingers to her lips in shock. She hadn't realized her time away from England had affected the way she spoke.

"Don't worry, I find the inflection charming," he promised. "The boy's is stronger, though."

"I will endeavor to diminish that as soon as possible. I want him to fit in."

"I'm sure he will," Hector promised. "Was his father from Scotland?"

"Yes, but we met at home."

"Where was home again?"

"My father's estate is to the south," she told him.

"That's right. I remember now. You have a sister who is newly out in society."

"You met Helen?"

He nodded. "At a ball. Clement introduced us, though I don't believe we danced."

Ruby rubbed her hands together, noticing her palms had become damp. She was anxious still about whether her sisters would accept her back into their company again but excited to hear anything of them. If her father really had disowned her, she might never know them again. What Ruby had done in running away might have reflected badly on them for some time. She hadn't considered that possibility until months later, when her letters to them had gone unanswered. "I haven't seen Helen since my marriage."

"She's lovely, but," Lord Stockwick smiled

slowly, "not as lovely as you, I think."

"You're very kind." Ruby's face warmed in a blush. "I hope the weather will clear soon. I should have liked to take Pip off for an adventure to see more of my grandfather's home."

"That's a fine idea." Hector stood. "Shall we go exploring together now?"

"I don't think we should go outside in this weather."

"Not out, but up and around," he said, twirling one finger about. "There's plenty to see inside The Vynes. How about we start upstairs in the nursery? Find the boy something new to play with."

Ruby was tempted, especially so when Stockwick gallantly held out his hand to help her rise. She slipped her hand in his and allowed him to bring her to her feet. There was a certain excitement in his gaze when their eyes met. Feelings she hadn't experienced in a very long time stirred in her belly. Not since her husband had she experienced anticipation and perhaps a not-so-innocent desire to be close to anyone. Ruby was definitely drawn to Hector which was ridiculous given how slight their acquaintance.

"A quick jaunt upstairs and then back here to warm up again," he promised with an eager smile, unaware of her inner thoughts.

Ruby's pulse quickened. "We could remain here and have tea instead."

"Only if you'll allow me to slip brandy into mine," he murmured, with a look she could only describe as seductive.

Ruby knew how other widows behaved with handsome men. For the first time, she understood their desire for a little attention too. In Scotland she would never have encouraged a flirtation. But she was in England now and bound to marry a man she might never have chosen for herself. She arched her brow. "How else do you drink it on a cold day?"

"Exactly." Stockwick grinned...and something inside her shifted again. It occurred to her that she was enjoying his company very much. She hadn't spoken to anyone so friendly since her husband had died, and she had certainly missed it. She hadn't been allowed to be herself in a very long time. Ruby Clement had run off to marry a man because of love. Ruby Roper could do as she pleased, too.

Ruby rushed to Pip and dressed him in his warm coat, soft cap, and scarf. "Time for an adventure, little man."

"Yay!" Pip cheered, jumping up and down.

Ruby rugged herself up, too, and they ventured out into the hall together. "If memory serves, the nursery is one floor up and to the east, isn't it?"

"That's right."

Taking her son's hand in hers, they climbed the steps together, with Lord Stockwick bringing up the rear. Inside was cold, and the vast room had obviously been deserted for some time, too. She brushed her fingers over the wood of a rail and came away with a thick layer of dust on her fingertips.

Everything she touched was the same, dirty

and uncared for, but Pip hardly seemed to notice. To his delight, he found toys belonging to his absent cousins to play with, and even a rag doll of a solider. He brought each discovery to Ruby, and she meticulously cleaned each one before allowing him to play with it.

Although it was cold in the nursery without a fire lit, she allowed her son to explore the chamber as long as he liked. She soon drifted to the window to look out at the view. The storm was still upon them. "I fear this won't end soon."

"Likely not," Stockwick agreed, coming to stand by her side. "We'll just have to make the best of it, use the time to get to know each other again."

She glanced up at him, wondering how much time they would have together. Her uncle wanted her to marry, and she didn't believe that he'd meant her to charm Lord Stockwick. But this might be her last chance to make peace with Hector over her lost silver bell. After she married, she may never come across him again. "I'd like that."

"Will you play with me?" Pip asked suddenly.

Ruby spun around from the scene outside —but it was to Lord Stockwick to whom her son had posed the question.

Stockwick went to the boy and peered down at what he was holding out. "What have you got there?"

"A horse. I found two of them."

"He's a fine-looking steed, isn't he?" Hector remarked, seemingly quite happy to indulge her son in conversation. To Ruby's surprise, he picked up the second horse and waved it about as if playing. Pip joined in, following Hector's movements but neighing, too.

Hector passed the second horse back to Pip then ruffled the boy's hair. "You'll take good care of them, won't you?"

"I will," the boy promised as he went back to his own game, galloping the toy about the room as if it were real.

She watched him for a few moments, her fingers at the base of her throat. Pip was so sweet and innocent and Hector so unexpectedly kind. She couldn't imagine life without Pip, and Ruby would do anything to give him the life he deserved. She hoped the man her uncle wanted Ruby to marry might play with Pip like this too.

"Gads, it's freezing up here." Hector left Pip and drew closer, rubbing his arms briskly. He was a very well-dressed gent, quite tall and slender, prosperous and at ease with himself around her. He smelled very nice too. She started blushing when he suddenly caught her eye and winked. "What's on your mind, Ruby Roper?"

That made her blush even hotter. She glanced at her son to hide his effect on her sensibilities. She ought not reveal her real thoughts to him. "I was wondering if anyone would notice if I borrowed a few things from the nursery to keep Pip amused until he can meet my cousins," she said, rather than the truth.

"I doubt anyone would care," he said, then

shivered. "Find what you need, and I'll help carry it all downstairs. Do it quickly before we catch our death."

Grateful for the distraction of the task and for his offer of assistance, Ruby rushed around gathering up slate and chalk, and a box of toys, and handed them off to Hector. Then she ushered Pip back downstairs into the warm parlor.

Stockwick delivered everything she'd gathered to Pip—and then pulled something brown out of his pocket.

She frowned at his hand. "Is that…"

"Mistletoe. Last year's pickings, I'm afraid. But still if one pretends it does the trick and offers an excuse for what I'm about to do next."

He held it up over her head—and then swooped in to deliver her first kiss since her husband had passed away.

For a moment, Ruby was quite shocked and didn't know what to do, but soon instinct took over, and she kissed him back.

They kissed for quite a while and then he drew back slowly. "That had to be better and longer than the first time I kissed you."

She frowned. "You've never kissed me."

"When we were children, I certainly did," he promised. "Right upstairs, outside the nursery we just visited. You were the first for me."

"I…" Ruby froze, startled that he even remembered that brief indiscretion. She'd been too young then to understand what he was about until much later. "So you did."

Hector smiled, his cheeks dimpling. "I was young then, and not very good at it most likely. The kiss we just shared was nice."

It certainly had been. Ruby could still feel the effect over her emotions, and her body, too. But she drew back from him. She shouldn't encourage him to imagine she'd fall into his arms every time there was mistletoe about. Her uncle expected her to behave, and her son was in the room.

Ruby turned toward Pip quickly, but he appeared to have noticed nothing that had gone on between her and Lord Stockwick. He wouldn't understand.

Lord Stockwick moved close behind but stopped short of touching her. She nearly shivered with the need to be held and kissed again. His nearness made her remember how close a couple could be. The press of a naked male body against her skin. The stroke of a hand along her inner thigh. She shook the memory away, blushing furiously.

Stockwick sighed. "I swear the next time I hold mistletoe over your head, it will be in a more private setting with no small person potentially listening or watching what we do," he promised. "Maybe then you won't feel as if you've betrayed him."

Before she could say she hadn't even thought of her husband, Hector went to the fire to play games with her son.

Ruby turned away to the window, confused by her feelings. Should she even feel guilty over a simple kiss delivered under mistletoe from a childhood friend?

Chapter Nine

HECTOR TOSSED the lad up over his shoulder. "Young man, you are in danger of becoming lost in all this snow," he warned.

Pip giggled, kicked his legs, then thrust out his arms wide. "Look at me! I'm flying!"

"Yes, but backward." Hector kept a firm grip on the boy as he trudged through the deep snow until they reached the stables, and then sat him down safely.

Pip was devilishly keen to see the horses today. Hector had seen the signs that his mother was fast losing her composure with the way Pip was carrying on inside and had offered to take the boy out to give her breathing space. Of course, the boy, unfamiliar with The Vynes, had run off immediately when they'd set foot outside and found the deepest patch of snow to become mired in. Hector had fished him out, and saved him from the next danger, too. Carrying him seemed the most expeditious way to get to where he wanted to go before they froze.

They quickly slipped into the stables and shut out the cold. The Vynes' stables were extensive and heated by regularly spaced, enclosed fires, but it was his men that Hector was interested in seeing first. He put a steadying hand on Pip's shoulders, so he didn't run off. "Hello," Hector called.

Twelve men suddenly appeared from the shadows from all parts of the stable. "Yes, my lord?"

"Franklin Jones?" he called out.

"Here, my lord." Hector's coachman pushed through the crowd. "Do you need the carriage made ready to leave?"

"Not in this weather. I wouldn't do that to you again so soon." Hector laughed. "Actually, what I have in mind is something that will require minimal effort on your part."

"We are at your service, of course."

Hector looked down at the boy. "Do you happen to know the location of a pile of clean hay the boy can jump about on? In?"

Franklin Jones grinned. "Indeed I do, and likely I have someone who might be very willing to join him, too."

He turned away, spoke to someone inside a chamber, and returned with a boy a few years older than Pip. The boy had an unusual scar across one side of his face and a wide smile.

"This is Allan. He'd be pleased to play with the young master for a while."

Allan rushed forward to claim Pip by the hand, and they ran off together to an empty stall.

Mr. Jones shrugged. "He's a good lad, but not too bright."

Hector kept track of where Pip went. "What happened to his face?"

"A horse kicked him when he was younger. It doesn't seem likely he'll ever grow up completely now."

"Ah," Hector said with a sigh. "That is unfortunate."

"A momentary distraction and the boy fell into harm's way. It happens all the time, but at least here, he'll always be cared for."

Hector heard Pip squeal and moved closer to the stall to see what was going on. The boy had straw on his clothes already and was reaching for another handful to throw up into the air.

Hector relaxed. "I'm surprised Lord Vyne was so generous as to house him."

Jones joined him. "He wasn't. Lord Vyne has little idea of what goes on beyond the great house anymore."

"So I gather," Hector said with a laugh as he pulled a small flask of whiskey from his coat pocket. "For your aches and pains. To help you sleep."

Jones beamed. "Thank ye."

Hector poked his head over the stable wall again, only to find Pip starting to tunnel into the hay pile. Young Allan raced around to the other side and started his tunnel, too. "They look to be well matched for their game."

Jones nodded. "Who is the young one?"

"I would have thought you knew more than I?"

"Never seen him before in my life."

"This is Lord Vyne's great-nephew. Mrs. Ruby Roper's son."

"Is that right? Hadn't heard anything about another relative come to stay."

That was odd. Servants always knew everything.

There was something about Ruby Roper that didn't sit right with Hector. It was strange how little she'd spoken of her life in Scotland. It was clear that she loved her son and thought well of her late husband, though. If Clement were here, Hector would ask him about his female cousin's marriage. As he was not, Hector was left to get his answers from the lady herself. It was unlikely that Vyne would tell him anything useful.

Hector allowed Pip a good amount of time to play and wear himself out, and then dressed him back into his warm and rather thin coat he'd thrown off. He hoisted Pip onto his shoulders for expedience and returned to the manor as quickly as he could walk that distance safely. Pip was a great deal more subdued when he greeted his mother in the upstairs parlor and happily returned to his toys to play.

She smiled. "Would you care for tea, my lord?"

"Yes, indeed, but only if you will call me by my given name when we are alone." Hector was on a first-name basis with all members of Meg's new family. It wasn't that scandalous, really, especially not here. "We are family now, in a way."

"I shouldn't do that."

"Well, the offer is made." He slipped another flask from his pocket, tipped some brandy into his cup—and Ruby's, too—and then sat back to sip his. "How long will you be staying at The Vynes?"

"I'm not certain," she said, eyes lowering to her cup.

He watched her mouth, became fascinated by the gentle curve and pout of her lips as she blew across the hot liquid. He thought of the pleasure of kissing her and if he might have another chance to kiss her again. The woman was indeed quite lovely, and he wanted to know all about what brought her here. He had a feeling it wasn't for a holiday. "Lord Vyne is not known for his generosity, even with his wife. I'm sure your visit here has an end date. My departure is imminent, I think."

Ruby's lips parted in surprise. "So soon."

"I came to see m'sister Meg. If she doesn't arrive soon, I will set off for Cornwall for our planned Christmas reunion." He smiled. "May I ask where you are bound for when you leave The Vynes?"

"Why?"

He smiled even more warmly. "Well, perhaps I should like to see you again."

Ruby glanced down at her hands. He noted the cup she held trembled as she put it aside. "I don't know where I'm going yet," she admitted.

Hector waited, hoping that if he gave her an opportunity, she might divulge her secrets.

She was wearing the same gown she'd worn for several days. The only dress he'd ever seen her wear was dated and fraying at the seams. Her marriage had not provided for her needs very well. He suspected she was in desperate straits and had come to her uncle hoping for his assistance. That could only be a mistake.

"What you say to me goes no further," he promised.

A tiny shuddering breath left her. "My husband died nearly a year ago. He was a good man, but he wasn't a wealthy one as you must have already determined. He was my father's servant. My father disowned me when it became known I had given my heart to someone of his lesser importance than expected."

Ah, she'd scandalized her family. He did remember hearing something about that but could not recall the finer details. "Most fathers react badly to scandals, I've noticed."

Ruby nodded. "I didn't care then because I had Liam. I went to live with my husband's family, but it soon became apparent they didn't care to have an Englishwoman in the family. Before I fled Scotland, Mr. Roper had decided I must marry a man I didn't know very well. He intended to keep Pip with him, so I had no choice but to run away from home. I took the mail coach, and then a series of carriages to reach The Vynes. I've asked for my uncle's protection."

A journey of weeks, perhaps, and costly, too. "I had assumed you hadn't any money. How did you pay for it all?"

"My mother-in-law had some money set aside. She gave it to me, and in return, extracted a promise to have Pip educated and to send him back when he'd reached his majority." Ruby glanced at the window. "Pip is the only family they have, too. I intend to honor that promise to Eliza Roper no matter what."

An unexpectedly kind gesture to a family that didn't want her. He admired her for taking steps to keep her son, and to avoid an unappealing marriage. Yet matrimonial peril not withstanding, her flight from Scotland would have been an anxious one for other reasons. "Do you fear Mr. Roper is in pursuit of you?"

She nodded. "I had had the good fortune to fall in love, but I ran off to be married without my parents' blessing. They did not approve of Liam. I was married over an anvil. I fear they will make me give up my son to Mr. Roper, and they might not protect me after the scandal I must have caused. That's why I came to my uncle first."

"Most likely, Vyne will write to your father and inform him of your location. Your father could bring Mr. Roper here, too."

"I'm sure they will come eventually." She chewed her lips. "I watch the drive all the time, in fear of losing Pip."

Having spent time with Ruby and Pip, he wouldn't want to see them separated, either. Male children were considered family property, though. That was the law. Women had few rights when it came to their offspring. Yet it felt wrong to allow any separation of Pip from his mother. Ruby would need a wealthy man to protect her. Lord Vyne was wealthy but not exactly the charitable sort. There had to be more to the story. "Why do you stay?"

"My uncle is still deciding how he can help me."

Most likely, Vyne was stalling. If it were up to Hector, he'd have spirited Ruby away to a distant abode and suggested she live a quiet life and for them to never use their real names again. "If Vyne refuses to help you, I will be only too happy to deliver you to your cousins in Cornwall or beyond."

"I'm sure that it will not be necessary, but thank you. My uncle has promised his assistance, but under a condition."

"How like him. What was his condition?"

"I am to marry a man of my uncle's choosing."

"Not you, too," Hector exclaimed in annoyance. "That is too high a price to pay for anyone."

"It is customary. Families arrange marriages for their daughters all the time. Don't say it isn't true. I need the protection of a marriage, my lord. Lord Vyne, no matter what he promises for Pip, will not live forever. I need someone with the power and funds for a bribe if necessary, to persuade Mr. Roper to leave Pip in my care."

Hector frowned, disliking the plan. Vyne should easily be able to support and hide, if necessary, two family members. Hector could do it without requiring Ruby to marry anyone. "I've heard Lord Vyne is expecting another guest to arrive soon. When did you make this deal with him?"

"The night I arrived. Do you think it could be the man he wishes me to marry?"

"It couldn't be. I arrived before you and I knew about the other guest coming that afternoon."

"Well, then it will be someone else he picks."

Someone Hector was sure not to like if they were closely acquainted with Lord Vyne. Surely Ruby didn't want to go along with all of this. "Are you sure you want to marry again? Like this?"

"No, of course I don't, but I have no choice." Ruby looked at him for a long moment. "I won't be parted from my son for any reason. I must do as my uncle wishes if Pip is to have the future he deserves."

"Well then," he murmured.

"Well then," she replied, her smile strained. "More tea?"

It really wasn't his place to tell Ruby what to do even if she was making a huge mistake trusting her uncle. "Hmm, I suppose that will do for now."

Chapter Ten

RUBY LIFTED her gaze to the view. The storm had passed during the night, leaving them with a blindingly white world. They would go outside today, see some of the estate at last. Hector had promised to be their guide. He had insisted on escorting them everywhere after her confession about a likely pursuit, claiming he didn't want them to become lost on the estate.

Ruby wasn't sure his company was in her best interests, but she felt safer with Hector around than without. He clearly hadn't approved of her plan to remarry to protect Pip, but he'd wisely kept his lips shut ever since voicing his initial objections. Pip seemed to enjoy his company immensely, too, and she was glad that Hector spared the boy some time.

When she saw the dark shape of a carriage approaching the manor through the swirling snow, her first thought wasn't about danger from Mr. Roper but the likely loss of her time alone with Hector. Eventually, though, she couldn't pretend she didn't see the distant carriage, and she pressed her hand to the cold glass to peer out.

"There's a carriage," she called finally.

Hector was suddenly at her back, looking out the window with her. "Do you recognize it?"

"No. Do you?"

"It's a wealthy man's carriage."

"Then it is not my father-in-law, unless he went to my father first, and together they've divined our location."

"It's too far away to tell still who it might be."

Hector's fingers stole around her waist, a light touch that made her turn. She was very nearly in his arms then—close but so far away. She thought of his offer for a second kiss and wet her lips in anticipation.

He smiled gently. "It will be all right, Ruby. I'll be right by your side, no matter who comes. I won't let them tear apart your family."

"Thank you," she whispered, feeling the frustration of her situation and regret. If not for her promise to her uncle, she might have taken that second kiss, and then perhaps a third, too, with no thought to the consequences.

Hector stepped aside.

Ruby immediately went to check her son, hiding her flaming cheeks. Pip could amuse himself while she was away for a little while greeting the newcomers. She had to know who was arriving. She needed to see who her uncle had chosen for her to wed—if that is who it was approaching.

Hector's footsteps sounded behind her. "Are you ready?"

"Yes, I'll just need my scarf." When she had it, she turned back to find Lord Stockwick helping her boy into his coat. "What are you doing?"

"Taking him with us."

"That's not a good idea." Pip was supposed to stay out of sight. "Lord Vyne might not like it."

"To hell with what he wants. If that's who you fear it might be, I'm not letting your boy out of our sight. Come on. There's no time like the present to confront your would-be oppressors," he announced.

"Oh," she said, chasing after him and Pip as they reached the door. "I hadn't wanted to put him in the middle of any argument."

Hector paused as he considered her words. "Then I will ask my valet to watch over him while we are gone. I'm sure he'd be only too happy to play with a few toys instead of pressing my cravats."

"That's very kind of you but not necessary," she promised.

"It is entirely prudent. You'll only worry otherwise." He jerked his head toward the door. "Come along, young Pip. I want you to meet my valet."

Her boy ran to Hector, a tiny toy horse clutched to his chest. Pip tugged on Hector's hand to make him look down. "Do you have a real horse?"

"Indeed I do. His name is Scout, but I'm afraid I had to leave him in London in his warm stable."

"My papa had a gray horse to pull his wagon."

"A wagon, you say," Hector repeated, and then smiled.

Ruby looked away. She hadn't married a

wealthy man, and by the time of his death, they'd lived a much simpler life than she'd ever imagined living. But Pip didn't know he should hide their lack of wealth and importance yet. She was grateful that Hector had accepted her tale and not chided her for following her heart, like her family had done.

Hector and Pip went down along the halls together, talking of horses and carriages. They stopped at a far door, and Hector spoke briefly to a man inside. The valet appeared and agreed to return Pip to the upstairs parlor to play.

She winced. "I won't be very long. Pip shouldn't need anything but watching."

"If it's all right with you, I'll ask for cake and milk to be sent up for the boy. Boys are always hungry. Take your time."

Hector took her arm. "Let's get us downstairs quickly. Dear God, The Vynes has always been a damn drafty place, and it seems worse this year."

"So you come here every year?"

"No. But I was here last year, and again a few years before that."

"I haven't been here since…

"Not since you lost your silver bell, I suppose. I wonder if we could find it this year."

She sighed.

"I do regret I tormented you as a boy. Moving the bell about the room when your back was turned wasn't very nice of me."

"You were sometimes very annoying," she murmured.

He shook his head. "I probably wanted to

make you notice me, chase me so that I could steal a second kiss."

She shook her head. "A scoundrel at just twelve years of age."

"Hmm, I probably was—and still am, depending on who you talk to," he admitted.

When she looked at Hector now, she saw a glimpse of that young boy but not much of the scoundrel he claimed to be. "But who else but you could have taken it from me?"

"I don't know. The last time I saw it, it was as I said then—beside your cot in the nursery, right before we all trooped downstairs to see our parents. The nursery was thoroughly searched for it the next day. The housekeeper made us all line up outside in our nightclothes. The servants quarters were thoroughly checked, too, I suspect."

"I asked the housekeeper when I arrived if it has ever been found, and she said not."

"I fear it is lost for good then, or it was taken by someone rather devious." He stopped her. "Have you been holding a grudge against me all this time?"

She blushed. "It was important to me. A keepsake from my paternal grandfather."

"I knew that then, too." He nodded and started moving again. "We could have been looking for it about the house these past few days. Put the matter to rest once and for all, eh?"

"I couldn't have troubled you," she said quickly.

"Nonsense. You know, I think I will be staying for Christmas after all. A scavenger hunt will be just the thing to keep us all warm."

"I can't ask you to change your plans for me."

He smiled quickly. "I wouldn't have changed my plans if I hadn't wanted to. Besides, I think Pip could do with the diversion of my company, and you, too."

"You might be right." Ruby blushed a little at Hector's kindness. He was staying for her, to protect her and Pip so they could stay together. If she had to marry anyone, Ruby wished it could be someone as gallant as him.

She had done a little snooping already for her lost item, but it might be a great help to have another set of hands to move a piece of furniture quietly, and Hector did seem quite strong. More muscular than her, at least, and taller. There were several high places quite beyond her reach in the library. "Lord Vyne might not like us poking about the house without his permission."

"Then I guess we'd better make sure he doesn't find out," Hector whispered.

They reached the front hall and heard the voices of men. Ruby hung back when Hector suddenly started to tiptoe to the library door, making no sound. He carefully peeked around the doorframe to look into the library—and then jerked back, shuffling a few yards in her direction. "Bloody hell," he muttered softly as he caught her elbow.

"What is it?"

"Samuel Blackwood is here."

"Who?" she whispered.

Hector ran a hand over his mouth and muttered, "A man you don't want ever to cross."

Judging by Hector's furtive behavior, he had.

And he was afraid of the man, too. Was he dangerous as well? Ruby wasn't keen to meet anyone who could make a grown man shrink in fear.

Ruby pulled at Hector by his sleeve, drawing him away from the library door and into the doorway of an empty reception room. "Go back upstairs. Quickly."

Hector shook his head. "There's no use delaying the meeting. He'll find out I'm here easily enough. Vyne will mention my name, of course."

That didn't sound good for Hector's sake. "What are you going to do?"

Hector tugged down his waistcoat. "Meet him and hope he doesn't plant me a facer."

Ruby frowned. "Why would he do that?"

"I kissed his sister."

"I thought you owed him money." Ruby rolled her eyes. "So you *are* a scoundrel."

"Well, she kissed me back," he exclaimed. "There was mistletoe!"

"Does that excuse all your indiscretions?"

"Especially those committed during the holidays." Hector grinned and held out his arm to Ruby. "Shall we introduce ourselves to Lord Vyne's important guest together, m'dear?"

Ruby considered taking it, but if there were punches to be thrown, she'd rather not be attached to Hector's side. However, if a lady were present, perhaps cooler heads would prevail. She pulled her shawl tighter about her shoulders. "I think we have no choice but to meet him together."

Hector leaned closer. "I never would have thought Vyne acquainted with the likes of Blackwood. He's hardly the sort to frequent country houses in the dead of winter unless there was something in it for him."

"I wonder what it could be?"

"No earthly idea, but I wonder if Lord Vyne owes the man, and Blackwood is here to collect an overdue payment."

"I suppose that might be it."

Hector drew close. "I guess our lovely afternoons upstairs, snug together, will have to wait until Blackwood departs."

Ruby frowned. Had he really enjoyed their company so much? "You've become a great favorite with Pip. He'll be disappointed."

"He's a clever boy, and his mother, too, has been a delightful companion." Hector teased his fingers up her arm. "I am glad we had a chance to meet again, Ruby. If not for Blackwood's arrival, you and I could have had a great deal more fun together this holiday."

"Fun?"

"Indeed." He smiled down at her as they walked along. "Don't deny you're not still thinking about our kiss, and my offer of a second."

A second kiss probably should never happen. She was starting to like Hector a bit too much as it was.

They reached the door side by side, and

Ruby immediately saw her uncle and a dark-haired stranger seated before the fire. Mr. Blackwood's face, when he turned in her direction, appeared hard. Ruby glanced at her uncle for guidance, and he smiled warmly at her.

Ruby edged a little closer to Hector.

Chapter Eleven

SAMUEL BLACKWOOD WAS a man of similar age to Hector, but taller and broader in the chest, and with fists that had bruised any number of scoundrel's faces. He owned a notorious gambling hell in London, which is where Hector had first encountered the man.

Meeting and kissing the man's sister had been a grave mistake on Hector's part. He'd had no idea who she was when they'd tangled tongues in Drury Lane Theatre. The last fellow who'd pursued the fetching Molly Blackwood with amorous intent was still taking all his meals in liquid form.

The only thing to Hector's advantage was that it had been only one kiss—well, two, since she'd kissed him back—and after learning her identity, Hector had never sought out Molly Blackwood again. He'd also given up gambling at Blackwood's establishment to avoid antagonizing the man.

But there was a chance that Molly Blackwood might have told her big brother all about him.

Well, he'd better get it over with and face his punishment like a man.

He strolled into the library with Ruby close by his side, hoping for the best. "Good morning," he called to both occupants of the room.

Ruby curtsied and murmured the same.

He noted that Lord Vyne did not rise to greet them, which seemed rude. "Ah, I was just about to send for you, Niece," Lord Vyne said to her. "Lord Stockwick."

"My lord." He bowed and then looked at Blackwood. "Sir. It's good to see you again."

Blackwood frowned. "I don't believe we are acquainted."

Hector was taken aback. "Lord Hector Stockwick."

Blackwood's face showed no recognition whatsoever. "A pleasure to meet you, my lord," he said.

Hector nodded. Could it be true that Blackwood did not recognize him? Was it also possible that Molly had not shared their encounter as well? "So, what brings you to Derbyshire?"

Blackwood smiled quickly and glanced at Ruby, a question in his eyes.

Lord Vyne smiled, too. "Ah, yes. Mrs. Roper, this is a very good friend of mine, Mr. Samuel Blackwood. Ruby is my brother's eldest daughter, and a widow. She has recently come to stay at The Vynes."

Hector noted Vyne did not mention Ruby had a son upstairs.

"A pleasure to meet you, sir," Ruby murmured, dipping the man a curtsy.

"The pleasure is all mine, I assure you," Blackwood promised.

"Do join us," Lord Vyne said. "You too, Stockwick. Sit yourself down over there."

Ruby perched at her uncle's side by the

fire, and Hector was relegated to a seat slightly farther away. Lord Vyne spared him just one glance and then directed all of his attention upon Blackwood and Ruby.

Hector didn't mind the cold shoulder. It gave him time to observe the excruciating politeness on display in front of him. Vyne was intent on ingratiating himself with Blackwood. It could only mean the earl owed Blackwood money, and it probably wasn't a trifling amount, either.

Vyne turned to Ruby. "Blackwood has been telling me he's taken possession of an estate not far from here," he told Ruby.

"Longlean," Blackwood murmured.

"A thousand acres of fertile soil and a grand manor to live in," Vyne claimed in tones of wonder and not a little envy.

Blackwood's lips twitched. "Not as grand as The Vynes yet, perhaps, but I do hope that one day people will think so. I intend to restore the estate and make my home there with my family."

"Yes, you have a sister, I believe." Hector sat forward, keen to end the suspense. Blackwood's expression didn't even flicker. "Restoring an estate in decline is a time-consuming and costly enterprise."

"Life has been good to me," Blackwood promised Hector but soon looked back at Ruby.

"What does your sister think of the place?" Ruby asked him.

Blackwood's jaw clenched momentarily. "My family are excited about the move, and my sister will particularly benefit from experiencing the slower pace of country life."

Hector quickly read between the lines. Blackwood would brook no opposition from his sister about the move, not if the woman wanted to enjoy his support in the coming years. Everyone whispered Molly Blackwood was well on her way to becoming as notorious as her brother. Blackwood was likely removing her from London to protect what remained of her reputation.

Hector wished the man all the luck in the world. He had tried to wrangle his sister Meg, for a different reason, in the same high-handed fashion when he'd brought Meg to The Vynes last year. A change of scenery had done Meg's glum mood the world of good.

"I'm sure they will love living there once they see the place," Ruby promised.

"Yes, an ambitious but achievable project for a man willing to exert himself for the good of the family," Vyne said in praise of Blackwood, then he turned to Hector, and his expression soured. "Something I understand you were not willing to do, since you sold your wreck of an estate to my son last year," Lord Vyne accused.

Hector was well aware that his interests and society's expectations clashed over his sale of the Cornwall estate. The place had simply not suited him. "I made a tidy profit from the transaction," Hector shot back with a satisfied smile. "And I made my sister happy in the bargain, since she lives there with Lord Clement even now."

Vyne scowled. "They should be here."

Hector shrugged. "Snow has never been my sister's favorite weather."

"Mine either," Ruby admitted softly. "Gentlemen, I am afraid you will have to excuse me."

"Of course." Blackwood rose, and Hector did, too.

"Very well." Vyne glanced at his pocket watch, nodded, but remained seated. "We will see you again at dinner tonight at seven o'clock, Niece. Wear something pretty to charm my guest."

"Of course, Uncle," she promised, and then directed a warm smile at Blackwood that Hector instantly coveted. "Until tonight, sir."

She merely inclined her head to Hector then left the room.

When Ruby's steps could no longer be heard, Hector sat again. Why had Ruby smiled so warmly at Blackwood?

When a servant brought spirits and started passing glasses around, Hector declined.

Lord Vyne smiled. "So, big changes afoot at Longlean."

"Indeed."

"You'll want a wife soon, too, I imagine," Vyne noted.

Hector straightened up in his chair, interested in seeing where this conversation would go next.

"Yes, people do say a wife will be necessary to bring Longlean back to life." Blackwood looked at the doorway. "I had already determined to do just that."

Blackwood didn't look enthused about the idea of making a marriage though. But every man with a fortune needed someone to inherit —even Hector would need a wife one day. To Blackwood, he said, "It seems everyone my age is in a hurry to shackle themselves to a ball and chain."

"Marriage is a means to an end," he answered. "Don't imagine living as a husband will change my nature very much."

"I'm keen to hear how you will avoid it?"

"How isn't important," Blackwood said, shrugging off Hector's question.

Vyne was nodding. "A match well made, connecting you to the right family, will ensure society opens its doors to you."

Blackwood nodded.

Vyne learned forward. "I could be of assistance."

Blackwood stared at Vyne. "Could you indeed?"

"Well, yes," Vyne promised.

"I must say I am intrigued."

Hector glanced down at his empty hands as Vyne gushed about his extensive list of acquaintances. The doors he could open for Blackwood. Hector did not like the sound of this alliance forming before his very eyes. Whoever Blackwood took as a wife would just be a means to an end for both men. Vyne's insistence on helping likely served his own purpose, too.

Once Blackwood had been accepted into society, his poor wife would no doubt be cast aside to a country estate—to be visited only to get an heir and a spare. It happened all the time in society, he knew, but it was the first time Hector had ever watched such a scheme unfold so coldly. He felt...unclean just being in the same room with them.

Hector stood. "Well, gentlemen. I think I must leave you now. Brave the cold and stretch my legs outside. Until dinner."

"Yes, dinner," Blackwood murmured. "I look forward to it very much."

Vyne said nothing.

Hector strolled from the room but he had no intention of freezing his balls off outside. He went directly upstairs, taking them two at a time, and stalked the halls until he found Ruby. She was in a bedchamber, a pretty evening gown laid out upon her bed. A dress meant to impress a suitor, and he wondered, too, if it was even hers. "What are you doing with that?"

"What? The dress?"

"Yes."

"I'm to wear it for dinner, I suppose. My uncle sent it along with several others this morning."

By the look of it the gown possessed a very low bodice meant to encourage a seduction. He recalled how Vyne had fawned all over Blackwood downstairs and felt sick. "You will not encourage that man's attentions by wearing that dress to dinner. I forbid it."

Ruby paused, and then moved toward him. She sighed as she looked up into his face. "I expected you to say something to that effect."

Faced with such a calm response to his outburst, Hector made an effort to control his temper. "He's not for you."

"Then who is? You?"

Hector snorted and took a step back. "That's not why I'm here."

She winced. "I know. I've known all along your interest in me is only an amusement. You've made your wishes quite plain but so have I. The needs of my life are not amusing, and they are no one's business but mine. I must marry to protect my son. Blackwood isn't married and it's plain to see he could deal with my father-in-law quite easily."

"He doesn't even know about Pip."

"But he will and once we become better acquainted, he might want to be a father to my son and help us stay together."

"Ruby let me—"

She patted his chest. "No, Hector. I do thank you for your company and your concern for our future. But please allow me to decide how best to protect my son."

"Blackwood isn't the man for you, or good enough to be a father to Pip. You're making a grave mistake."

She shook her head. "Please don't ruin this opportunity for me, Hector. Blackwood might just turn out to be the man of my dreams."

"Or your darkest nightmare," Hector muttered under his breath.

Chapter Twelve

SAMUEL BLACKWOOD WAS a hard man to draw into a conversation, but Ruby tried her best. She and her uncle were sitting in the conservatory surrounded by potted palms the next morning and struggling through a discussion on the latest scandals. The room was so well heated, Ruby could hardly stand it. She desperately wished for a fan with which to cool her face.

Of Hector, she'd seen no sign this morning. He'd taken her interest in Blackwood to heart and absented himself from socializing. That was a pity, for she was sure his presence might have helped lighten the mood in this room considerably.

"More tea, Uncle?"

"Yes, I think I will." Lord Vyne held out his cup, his attention on her, and he nodded as she poured.

Ruby took that to mean he was pleased with her and with her attention to Blackwood so far. The only thing that rankled was Vyne's insistence she could not introduce or mention her son to Blackwood still. It seemed a ridiculous restriction.

She passed her uncle his cup. "My lord."

"Thank you, my dear."

Uncle Vyne had begun speaking more sweetly to her as well since Blackwood had arrived and they'd been introduced. He made it seem like he was a benevolent, even affectionate relative. "Mr. Blackwood, would you care for a second cup?"

"No, thank you."

Blackwood was strictly a one-cup-of-tea man and an impatient one. He often started tapping his foot when her uncle began droning on about their family.

She put the teapot down, having no interest in drowning in tea herself. After folding her hands in her lap, she looked to her uncle.

Vyne was watching Blackwood. "Have you had a chance to tour the manor, Mr. Blackwood?"

"Not as yet."

Ruby did not blame the man. The Vynes' public rooms seemed only a few degrees above freezing on most days.

"Mrs. Roper, if you would be so good as to give our guest a tour in my place."

Although surprised by the unexpected request, Ruby inclined her head. "I'd be happy to."

She knew little about the contents of the many rooms at The Vynes, but she supposed extolling the virtues of Lord Vyne's home was not what her uncle had in mind. She had been instructed to woo Mr. Blackwood.

After dinner on the night she'd met Blackwood, her uncle had sent for her and explained the extent of his help. He owed Blackwood a debt that he believed her attentions to the man would fulfill. Marriage was the only outcome Ruby would insist upon. She would not be used for her body, pimped to Blackwood as a whore just to set the earl free. And in exchange for her involvement in her uncle's scheme, she'd demanded he answer her questions—no matter how uncomfortable.

He'd said Lady Vyne and his children had humiliated him by leaving to live in Cornwall, and he also admitted that the strength of his legs had become unreliable—which was why she'd never seen him standing. And why he stayed in his rooms most of the time.

She felt sorry for him in a way, but he reminded her of Mr. Roper. He intended to use Ruby to have his way unless she stood up for herself.

Ruby stood, picked up the coat and scarf she'd discarded upon entering the conservatory and led the way out. As soon as she encountered the cold, she quickly slipped on her coat and wrapped her scarf about her neck, too.

Blackwood, absent a coat, rubbed his arms briskly. "Is it always so chilly here?"

"I believe so."

She led Blackwood toward the heated drawing room, where there were a few portraits she recognized. She pointed at one. "My uncle and my father with their parents, in their youth."

Blackwood squinted at all the faces in turn. He drew back, one brow raised. "People always appear so perfect in these sorts of things."

Ruby almost laughed. The painting showed nothing of the reality of her father. "If I could afford to commission an artist to immortalize my family, I'd want to look my best, too."

Blackwood studied the painting again, but this time only the artist's signature scrawled across the bottom corner.

When he'd finished, he held out his hand, urging her to continue their stroll.

She took Blackwood through the dining room and then the long hall, noting that every fire in the house had been lit today. Vyne must have ordered it done, intending to seem a generous and considerate host to Blackwood.

The long hall held many grand paintings, but Ruby hardly knew one from the other. They walked in silence for the length of the hall.

When they stopped, it was at a far window. The view outside was white still, but the snow was no longer falling. If not for her bargain with her uncle, she and Pip might have gone exploring together today.

Blackwood turned to her. "Not much excitement out there."

"The Vynes is a place of peace and tranquility."

"I'd much rather the chaos of London," Blackwood admitted.

"My family has a house in London, too." A place she might never see again unless she married well and they invited her back into the fold.

"Mayfair is not the real London," Blackwood warned. "I shouldn't think you'd find it much to your liking."

"Why is that?"

"London is unruly, disorder and chaos. Loud and unapologetic. It requires a certain degree of flexibility and dishonesty that I suspect you entirely lack."

Ruby found his statement both pleased and angered her. How dare he assume to know her character on so brief an acquaintance? He didn't know anything about her, really. Lord Vyne would hardly have told him the truth. She could enlighten Blackwood here and now but found she didn't want to, no matter what she'd promised her uncle. "I guess I'll never know until I see it for myself."

She moved along the hall a ways, to a new window with a slightly different view. What was she to do about Blackwood and that promise to her uncle? Perhaps she should have taken up Hector's offer of assistance the moment he'd spoken of it. They could have been halfway to Cornwall by now. She needed very little but safety, and a little warmth, too.

To her surprise, she saw him, Hector, trudging through the deep snow...with a small bundle thrown over his shoulder. When the bundle wriggled, kicking tiny legs and arms, she froze in surprise.

Hector had her son and was taking him off to the stables.

At the door, Hector set him down and straightened his clothing.

Pip looked up at Hector, clearly talking his head off, and Hector ruffled his hair before pushing open the door.

They disappeared, clearly off for another adventure without her.

She had not expected Hector to seek to entertain her son again today, or any day. Not after she'd made it plain she would not kiss Hector again. But Pip did love horses, and the stables were his favorite place in the world.

She found Hector's interest in her son surprisingly pleasing.

Blackwood drew close. "Is something wrong, madam?"

"No. The view is just like all the rest. I am just a little chilled."

"I am too." He bowed to her. "Thank you for showing me more of the house. If you will excuse me, I should like to return to Lord Vyne and continue our earlier conversation."

"But of course. Thank you, Mr. Blackwood, for your company. It has been a pleasure to become better acquainted with you."

As soon as he left, Ruby hurried for a rear door, looking for a well-trod path to take her to the stables. It wasn't hard to find the path Hector must have taken. His footprints were deep, though, and she quickly understood why Hector might have thrown Pip upon his shoulder.

She carefully picked her way through the snow, using Hector's footprints to spare herself the worst of the cold and damp. But by the time she reached the stables, her toes were cold and her stockings were wet.

She pushed the heavy door open and instantly saw Hector leaning against a stall not far away. He looked over his shoulder, and then snatched up a blanket before hurrying to her. "What are you doing coming out in this weather?"

"I saw you and Pip coming here."

"He's playing."

She didn't see Pip. "Where?"

Hector wrapped her in the blanket and, with one arm around her back, propelled her to the stall he'd just left.

Pip was inside, marching around the stall with another, larger boy. They were stomping down the hay beneath their feet and laughing their heads off. Pip's cheeks were pink already, and he was smiling. The other boy was just the same.

Ruby drew back but was worried. "If my uncle saw him doing that, he might not approve."

"It's harmless play. And the straw is clean, intended only to thicken the mattresses of the stable hands. They just hadn't gotten around to using it yet and don't mind. Young Allan there does this all the time, I'm told."

Relieved, she glanced around the stables. There were no servants anywhere about. Only Hector, watching the boys play together.

Hector's arm stole around her again. "Are you warm enough?"

"My feet *are* a bit cold," she admitted.

"Well, then," Hector said as he pulled her a little tighter to his side. "Shall we stroll the stables to keep ourselves warm? While we do, I suggest we make a game of choosing more fitting names for Lord Vyne's horses. Vyne, I've found, lacks the imagination to choose names worthy of such handsome steeds."

She laughed. "I've never named a horse before."

"Well, now is your chance to try while we pass the time waiting for Pip or Allan to tire themselves out."

She looked back toward her son.

Hector squeezed her waist, and then released her. "Don't worry. Given your confession the other day, I took the liberty of making sure he's being watched at all times."

When he pointed up, Ruby spotted a pair of stable hands in the hayloft directly above Pip, sitting with their legs dangling over the side.

"You didn't have to do that. Pip is not yours to protect."

He looked away, frowning. "Clement would expect me to make sure his cousins remained safe at all times."

Ruby didn't quite believe Hector's claim that he was standing in for Lord Clement. Hector cared about Pip.

And he might just care about her, too.

Pleased by that, Ruby withheld a smile as she took Hector's arm, and they moved to the closest stall.

The differences between Hector and Mr. Blackwood were quite marked. Blackwood's character was evident on his face. He'd be a dangerous man to cross, as Hector claimed.

And while Hector might declare himself a scoundrel, and quite proudly, too, he was a great deal warmer and kinder than he liked to let on. He was impulsive, boastful, but even though she'd told him of her interest in

Blackwood for marriage, he was still willing to go out of his way to ensure her son's safety.

She already knew which man might make her a better husband. The only impediment to her hopes was whether Hector would ever realize it, too.

Chapter Thirteen

DINNER THAT NIGHT was an unusually long affair hosted by Lord Vyne himself in lavish style. He appeared to be in a merry mood, indeed. The smile he wore tonight instantly gave Hector pause. He was gregarious, expansive, and keen to foster any conversation involving Ruby and Blackwood trading confidences.

Hector was feeling left out long before the dessert course was set before him. His part of the conversation had amounted to very little, since most frequent topics seemed to be rural pursuits and family connections. He looked down at his bowl of brandy custard and discovered that not even a favorite food could cheer him up.

Ruby laughed. "I should have liked to see that," she promised Blackwood before tucking into the custard with undisguised relish. She licked her lips. "Hmm, delicious."

Hector lost all discontent in the evening then and there. He couldn't take his eyes away from the glossy shine of Ruby's lower lip. He wanted to lean over the table, kiss those pretty lips, and whisk her away from everyone.

In all of his liaisons with pretty women, Hector had not once felt quite so desperate to have a woman all to himself as he did Ruby. He didn't know her well, but he wanted to know her better than anyone that had ever lived. Better than her late husband had, certainly, and better than her son.

For a man who routinely avoided entanglements, he found the prospect of an intimate, more profound connection with Ruby Roper didn't scare him in the least.

He finished his custard and declined to partake of anything more to eat or drink. As a group, they left the dining room. Vyne tottered instead of strode, leaning heavily on a footman, and Ruby and Blackwood followed side by side, which left Hector to bring up the unhappy rear on his own. When they seated themselves around the fire, Hector again found himself on the outside, pushed back from the woman he'd rather be closer to.

Blackwood began regaling Ruby with stories of his lifelong escapades in London—highly sanitized, Hector decided—to make her laugh. It was clear she was enjoying Blackwood's company more than his tonight. She had hardly looked at him all night and he missed having her attention.

It occurred to Hector that he could push himself forward, make a definitive step toward singling Ruby out for notice—remind her of the heat of their earlier kiss. But no matter how promising that kiss might have been, Hector was mindful of the fact that Ruby's interest was in achieving a marriage, not a brief dalliance that might cause a scandal.

If he chose to pursue this woman, he could not have any doubts that he was headed toward becoming a husband, and a father to her young son. Not a decision to make lightly.

The way things seemed to be going with Blackwood, she was well on her way to charming the man into falling in love with her. But Blackwood had not yet met young Pip, so it remained to be seen if a child made a difference to Blackwood's interest in the end.

Ruby and Pip had both charmed Hector. He could certainly offer them everything Blackwood could and more, since he held a title. Ruby could once again be welcomed by society and any estrangement with her family might end, too, if that was what she wanted. The boy would certainly benefit, though indirectly, from a connection to the Stockwick title. Hector would never skimp on the boy's education and upkeep—*if* he married Ruby, that was.

If.

Hector made an excuse and left the room, mulling over his future and his interest in Ruby.

Despite his claim of relishing his bachelor status, there had been times when having someone around made him happier than being alone. He had been eager to see his family this holiday, yet despite Meg not having arrived yet, he was not unhappy.

Ruby was a delightful woman. Pretty and calm. He'd enjoyed the time they'd spent together. There was not a hint of shrew anywhere about her. And he did like young Pip and wanted good things for him.

He absolutely did not want Pip taken away to Scotland and separated from his mother.

Hector reached the top of the stairs and turned when he heard a commotion coming from the family wing. Two men emerged from a chamber.

Caught between them, and struggling, was Pip.

Hector raced down the hall. "Unhand that boy!"

The men saw him but still tried to get away with Pip. Hector chased them down before they reached the servants' stairs, and forced them away from the boy by punching both in the nose.

Pip was dropped, and Hector did his best to cushion his fall and gather him up. He hefted the crying boy into his arms and held him tight as he backed away from the boy's would-be assailants, one fist still raised. "Don't you dare try anything against me. Who the hell are you to touch my son?"

Hector blinked even as the men advanced on him. Apparently Hector had decided to be Pip's new papa, after all.

He slid Pip behind him and raised both fists, ready to defend his new family from all comers.

But he soon wasn't alone in the hall. Alerted by the commotion, Parker was suddenly between Hector and Pip's assailants. Parker grabbed one fellow by the throat and banged him into the paneled wall. "My employer asked you a question. Answer him."

The fellow, a bit larger than Parker,

struggled and fought. "We were only doing what we were paid to do!"

Hector picked Pip up into his arms, aware the poor boy had been frightened badly and was shaking like a leaf now. "By whom?"

"We were to take the boy. That's all I know."

But someone had hired them. And a servant below stairs must have let this pair in and showed them the way to the boy's chamber. "Take him where?"

"Don't know, but there's a carriage waiting in the woods to take him the rest of the way."

"The boy won't be going anywhere." Hector held out one hand, fingers clenched in a fist still. "Come near this boy again, and I'll do worse than bloody your nose. Don't ever let me see your face again!"

The second man, obviously believing Hector meant every word, started inching down the hall away from them all, clutching his nose.

Although Hector would prefer to question them further, they were just pawns, and the boy was his priority. "Let him go, Parker."

Parker released the fellow he'd held by the throat and straightened up slowly. The men turned and fled for the servants' staircase; they shoved at each other as they made their escape.

When they were gone, Parker turned back to Hector. "Is the boy all right, my lord?"

"I've no idea yet." Hector turned on his heel and stalked to his chambers. Pip's grip tightened on his neck as they entered the room, and Hector sat down with him. "It's all right, my boy," he whispered. "I won't let them touch you again. Let me look at you, son. Are you hurt?"

"My arm," Pip said, sobbing softly.

Parker came to kneel at Hector's feet. "May I see your arm, lad?"

Pip's grip on Hector eased, and he showed Parker his arm with obvious reluctance. Hector held his breath as his valet carefully inspected the child's hand, wrist, and forearm. "I don't think it serious, but perhaps it should be wrapped for the night just in case."

Hector held Pip a bit tighter against him, seething with anger that perhaps the servants at The Vynes had conspired to take Pip away from him and Ruby. "Do it yourself. Do not involve The Vynes servants."

Hector sat back, holding the boy snug against him. He felt protective of the boy now more than ever. Hector dropped his chin to the boy's head. "I won't let anyone take you away from your mama or me."

Pip's grip on his neck tightened. "Where is she?"

"Still at dinner." He didn't relish telling Ruby that The Vynes was not the haven she'd believed it to be. "I'll fetch her."

Pip grabbed him, shaking like a leaf. "No! Don't leave me," he cried.

"I'm not going anywhere yet," Hector promised, even rocking the boy in his arms a little in the manner he'd noticed Ruby do on occasion. His heart swelled with tenderness for the boy, and with fear, too. What if he'd not come upstairs when he had? Pip might have been miles away before the abduction had been discovered.

Parker returned, his hands full of pristine white pressed linen cravats ripped in half. "It's the best I can do."

"A sacrifice for a worthy cause," Hector promised, ruffling the boy's hair and making him sit up for Parker.

Pip's wrist was bound firmly. "He needs rest, my lord," Parker suggested.

Pip just about strangled Hector out of fear of being separated.

"It's all right, my boy. You can stay here and sleep in my bed tonight. Parker will be with you every moment. I will have to leave you to fetch your mother. Do you still want her?"

"Yes, but I want you, too," Pip whispered, and his grip on Hector remained desperately keen.

Although it took a while, Parker finally managed to lure Pip out of Hector's arms with the promise of a story. The boy was taken to the bed, encouraged to lie down under the sheets and blankets, and then Parker pulled up a chair beside it.

Hector paused at the foot of the bed, watching Pip as he wriggled and fidgeted in the strange surroundings as Parker made up a story on the spot. The boy was probably still frightened, but Hector turned down the lamps a little to encourage him to drift off.

Then he returned to the bed and ruffled Pip's hair. "Close your eyes now, my lad. We'll have a big day tomorrow—just you and me and your mother, and Parker, too. Perhaps we'll go for a carriage ride together. Wouldn't that be grand?"

Pip nodded.

Hector paused beside Parker. "Lock the door after I'm gone, just in case someone comes looking for the boy again. Don't let anyone know he's in this room."

"No one will get past me, my lord," Parker promised and continued his story of a young boy who found a stallion in the woods and rode far and wide, having the greatest of adventures.

Chapter Fourteen

RUBY HAD PERHAPS ENJOYED TOO much wine with dinner. The warm room and company had been delightful. It could only have been greatly improved though if Hector had returned to join them. She sincerely wished he had come back. There was nothing better than enjoying a good laugh with him.

But Blackwood had been unexpectedly good company tonight, and her uncle, too, for that matter. Although he did keep making remarks that could only be considered matchmaking attempts. He extolled her virtues, accomplishments, and musical talents, some of which she hadn't pursued since the day she had married Liam. There hadn't been too many opportunities to play the harp or perform the Cotillion in the wilds of Scotland. The Ropers hadn't been much for frivolous amusement of any sort, really.

She stood, wobbling slightly. "Gentlemen, I'm afraid I shall have to excuse myself. It has been an enjoyable evening."

Vyne glanced at his pocket watch, frowning. "Yes, certainly. Do retire for the night, by all means."

"Good night, Uncle. Mr. Blackwood," Ruby said as she dipped a curtsy to both.

Blackwood stood, too. "I think I will turn

in as well. Vyne, you set a good table. I hope our business allows a repeat one day."

Ruby swept from the room, hoping not to have Mr. Blackwood follow her too closely.

Blackwood did follow her a little way, at a distance, but then turned for his guest room and disappeared inside.

Relieved, Ruby let herself into her chamber and yawned. "I'm back, love," she whispered, just in case Pip was still awake.

"Good," Hector said from behind her. "I was starting to think I'd have to come find you."

Ruby turned, startled to find Hector emerging from behind her bedchamber door. "What are you doing here?"

She glanced at the bed, startled to see it had been remade neatly. When she'd gone down for dinner, Pip had been sitting up in her bed playing with his toys, and a maid had been meant to watch him until he fell asleep. They were both gone. "Where is Pip?"

Hector came forward. "Now, I don't want you to be alarmed."

"And now I am. Where is Pip?"

Hector took both her hands in his. "He is in my room with Parker watching over him. He should be fast asleep by now."

Instead of being reassured, Ruby only grew more alarmed. "Why is he there?"

"Come and sit down with me," Hector asked, and she let him press her down into a chaise close to the fire. "There has been an incident. I came upstairs to find two men emerging from this room with Pip held between them. I made them release him, and they wisely fled."

"Dear God, Mr. Roper has found us." Ruby gasped and sprang to her feet. "Is Pip all right?"

"A little shaken up, and he has a sore wrist that Parker bound. He fought to be free of them taking him, and then I helped him."

She gaped. "You protected my son?"

"Indeed, I did." Hector rubbed his knuckles, and she saw they were reddened. "Those men say they were acting on orders and I doubt they will be back tonight."

Ruby reached for Hector's hand immediately, grateful for his quick thinking and intervention. "I want to see my son!"

"Of course," Hector promised without hesitation. "Come with me."

Hector opened the door carefully and, after leaning out to check the hall was clear, he drew Ruby outside with him. He led her down the hall to his chamber, knocked rapidly, and they waited for what seemed like an eternity to hear footsteps inside.

"What do you want?" Parker demanded, sounding cross.

"It's Stockwick," Hector replied.

"And Mrs. Roper," Ruby whispered, too.

The door was immediately unlocked and opened wide to admit them. Ruby rushed inside and went straight to the bed, where her boy lay sleeping.

She smoothed his hair back from his face

then found his bound wrist under the blankets. Pip whimpered in his sleep then settled back into slumber.

Ruby exhaled slowly, relieved she still had her son. But she was also afraid. Mr. Roper had a mean temper when he didn't get his way. And he'd found her so quickly she was reeling. He'd certainly return for another attempt to take the boy. She turned to share her suspicions with Hector, but he appeared in deep conversation with his valet.

"Have there been any movements of servants past this room?" Hector asked.

"No, my lord," the valet promised. "It's been quiet."

Ruby let out a relieved breath but that didn't mean the danger wouldn't return.

"Good. Let's be sure it will remain that way. Go downstairs and fetch me a glass of milk."

Parker raised a brow. "Milk, my lord?"

Hector scowled at him. "All right, not milk, but you know what I mean. Ask for another bowl of warm custard, perhaps. Anything. Find out if they know anything about those men. Try to find out who was involved and if they are coming back. I don't care to be surprised again."

"A very good idea."

Parker slipped from the room, and Hector was suddenly at Ruby's side, his hand outstretched. She gripped him tightly. "How could strangers get past every servant in the house and into my room?"

"I don't know."

"Wherever we go, Mr. Roper will find us? I can't lose Pip."

"You won't."

"Where can we go that is safer than here?"

"Anywhere would be better, I should think." Hector squeezed her hand tighter in his. "We'll leave tomorrow and make plans for our final destination on the journey."

"You don't have to go with us," she warned.

Hector leaned down and whispered into her ear, "You're not going anywhere without me tagging along to keep you safe now."

"We could go to my cousin in Cornwall," she suggested.

Hector dropped a kiss to her hair. "Clement is supposed to be on the way here, remember. But with luck, we might meet him en route and seek his counsel about all this first."

Hector pulled Ruby up, sat down in her place, and then settled her onto his lap. He cuddled her close and Ruby clung to him. If not for Hector retiring early, Pip might have been miles away.

"I imagine Pip is safe for the time being."

"I can't stay here," she agreed.

"We'll have to stay until dawn. Blundering about on a dark snowy night would be just as dangerous."

Ruby stared at her son even as she snuggled deeper into Hector's arms. Pip was so innocent and fragile. "I'd be so afraid if not for your calm and strength tonight," she whispered to Hector.

"I'm here for you."

It was more than an hour later when Parker returned, slipping into the room using the room key. Hector was relieved to see him at last. "Where have you been?"

Parker winced. "The servants hall was in an uproar. I honestly don't think they had any idea about those men coming in, but they certainly took great pains to chase them away. They were followed and shot at, I heard. I don't believe those particular men would dare return tonight, not unless someone paid them very well."

Hector shrugged. "Unlikely they'll return tonight but tomorrow…"

Tomorrow could see more men come to take the boy. It would be over his dead body.

"The butler was storming around, checking all the locks as I came up and berating everyone who got in his way. I was questioned, too, and warned to be vigilant. I didn't let on about the boy's near abduction, as you warned me not to say anything."

"Good." Hector rose, sliding Ruby off his lap to stand. He brought Ruby's hand to his lips and kissed the back of it. "Mrs. Roper and her son will be leaving first thing in the morning."

Ruby looked at him with wide, frightened eyes. "Without you?"

"With me, too," Hector promised her. "I'm

afraid I might never let either of you out of my sight again." He kissed her hand again, but she moved closer. "I've been thinking about what we talked about the other day. About what you want and need. I want to spend Christmas with you and Pip. I want you, and Pip, too, to have the time to decide if I'm worthy of being part of your lives."

"That statement only goes to prove that you are." She leaned in to kiss his cheek. "Your actions have forever placed us in your debt."

"I don't want that, but I do want to be the man who protects you."

She burrowed into his arms. "You know, you are not the scoundrel you make yourself out to be, my lord."

He smiled. "I suspect my days as a scoundrel might be done."

"Poor Hector. Perhaps you could be a little scandalous every now and then."

"Now there's an idea. I could happily spend my life seducing you," Hector mused, a slow smile lit up his whole face.

"A lifetime? Do you mean that?"

Hector leaned down and rubbed his nose against hers. "I do."

But then he became aware that Parker was clearing his throat loudly. Hector glanced at the man. "Is something the matter?"

"I was thinking that I could stay by the boy's side tonight while you and Mrs. Roper finished planning your future together."

"That's not…" Hector began.

"… a bad idea," Ruby finished. "Thank you, Parker. Pip would normally sleep until morning but if my son wakes before we return, we will be just down the hall in my room. I have a few items to collect to take with us tomorrow."

Hector nodded. "Yes. You stay here with the boy, keep the door locked, and we'll be back to make arrangements for our departure before morning comes."

"Very good, my lord," Parker promised.

Hector turned to Ruby and ushered her out into the hall. All was silent as they made their way to her room and let themselves in.

"This will only take a moment." Ruby moved about in the dark, collecting things and stuffing them in a satchel.

Hector could not wait to take Ruby and Pip away from here. Somewhere he could be assured of their safety.

It troubled him how fast Mr. Roper had found the estate, though, if Pip's abduction had been by Roper's hand at all. How could the man have deduced Ruby would have ever come to her uncle so quickly? How could Roper have afforded to hire those men if they were not well off?

Those doubts made him now wonder if the real culprit behind the abduction attempt was wealthy, much nearer to hand and devious to the bone.

Hector put his arm around Ruby protectively as another likely explanation occurred to him.

Ruby turned in his arms and before he could voice his suspicions, she rose up and pressed her lips to his. The kiss took him by surprise, but it was not unwanted.

He had thought of kissing Ruby again and if they were going to be together, he looked forward to a great many more such exchanges.

She drew back. "When you have a child, you will discover you must take advantage of every moment of solitude for pleasure."

"I've always been a fast learner."

He swooped in to kiss her back, and when she looped her arms about his neck, her next kiss promised endless pleasures. When her tongue teased past his lips to tangle with his, Hector drew Ruby closer, delighted that they had found each other again.

Hector drew back. "Tomorrow, I must speak with your uncle."

"We don't need his permission," she promised. Her hands slid down to his chest, and he was nudged back toward the bed firmly. "In fact, since I'm a widow, I don't have to listen to anyone at all again. No one but you. Now, let me tell you what I think we should do before we return to my son. And I hate to say that some haste will be required tonight."

Ruby quickly divested herself of her attire and Hector quickly understood. Hector grew hard as her pretty breasts and curves were suddenly within reach of his eager fingers.

Ruby pushed him onto his back on her bed and climbed atop him. She lifted her hands to her hair and released it from its confines.

Soft, long locks fell over his hands and tumbled down around them. He grasped a handful, then tossed Ruby over onto her back. "Lovely woman, now I'll *never* let you go."

"No more talking." Ruby drew him down for a kiss and further conversation became completely unnecessary.

Chapter Fifteen

A NIGHT of lovemaking hadn't improved Hector's temper very much. He shut the door to Vyne's study in the hope of keeping Ruby from finding where he'd gone too soon. He didn't want her to hear what he had to say to her uncle.

"You unfeeling bastard," Hector growled.

Lord Vyne's head snapped up from the papers he'd been reading on his desk. "I beg your pardon."

"Don't pretend. You just couldn't for once be a decent human being." Hector spared a single glance for Blackwood, but Vyne was the one he wanted to gut right now. He'd pondered the sudden abduction attempt all night and concluded Mr. Roper simply did not have the ability to abduct his own grandson without help. Vyne had to be behind the abduction himself. "How could you try to send Pip away from her?"

Lord Vyne, seated still, put his hands on the arms of his chair. "I don't know what you're talking about."

Lie. "You waited till dinner when the servants were busy below and used Blackwood as a distraction to keep Ruby away from the child."

Blackwood rose from his chair. "What child?"

"Ruby has a son, born within a marriage the family never approved of. While you were being charmed after dinner, Blackwood, I returned upstairs, only to be confronted by two assailants. They were trying to abduct Ruby's boy. I would bet they were here on *his* orders."

Vyne's face mottled red.

Blackwood moved to stand by Hector's side, looking down at the earl with disdain. "I don't recall you ever mentioning Mrs. Roper's offspring. In fact, you implied she was unencumbered."

"Vyne likely thought the existence of the boy would scare you off."

"I like children."

"Enough to become a father to Pip?"

"No, I am not in a position to do that. Not for anyone," Blackwood admitted. He folded his arms over his chest. "Now I understand why he kept throwing his niece at me instead of discussing when he'd be paying off his debt."

"One has nothing to do with the other, I assure you," Vyne promised. "Not that I was involved in any abduction."

"Most likely, he wished to lessen his debt somehow by joining your family to his, delaying talks of any repayment to you for quite some time."

Blackwood scowled. "Lord Vyne, I shall have to decline any delay to that repayment. I will accept full payment by luncheon today, and then I will be on my way. My *wife* is expecting me to reach home by Christmas Eve."

Vyne gasped. "You're married?"

"For some time, and I already have children. Six," Blackwood promised.

Hector couldn't help but laugh at Vyne's shocked expression. "Congratulations. Six children and a wife, too. Imagine that."

"Twin's. Three sets of boys," Blackwood said proudly. "I've kept my family far away from London and what goes on there, but they'll be moving to the new estate soon."

"How marvelous," Hector exclaimed and it was the best news he'd ever heard.

Lord Vyne's face was slowly turning purple and that was good, too.

"Congratulations to you, too," Blackwood murmured. "I think Mrs. Roper will make an excellent wife for someone who can appreciate her best qualities and protect them."

Hector nodded. "I'm sure she will marry well, and soon. But first, I need to make sure her uncle understands the error of his ways."

Blackwood slapped Hector's shoulder. "Do me a favor—don't kill him. I can't get money out of a dead man."

"Oh, he'll live, but not happily, I should think."

"Oh, and while we're confiding in each other—stay away from my sister once you marry. My sister is a complication you do not want in your life," Blackwood suggested with a bland smile.

Hector had nearly forgotten all about kissing Blackwood's sister. "I assure you, I will keep a distance," he promised. He was done with all women—except Ruby.

He waited until Blackwood was gone before he faced Lord Vyne again. The man seemed decidedly uncomfortable and blessedly silent. Good. Hector had a few things to get off his chest. "For years, I've watched you manipulate those around you with no thought to their happiness."

"The concerns of my family are no business of yours," Vyne snapped.

"That's where you are very wrong. I'm connected to your family now. My sister is about to deliver Clement's first child."

Vyne's eyes were wide. "A grandchild?"

There was complete wonder in Vyne's voice. Hector narrowed his eyes. "Well. Well. Well. Didn't you know about the coming babe?"

Vyne sat up a little straighter. "No. My son is neglectful in his duties and failed to inform me."

"I'm not surprised you're the last to know." He smiled coldly at Vyne. "Do you imagine Clement will allow you to spend any time with your grandchildren once he learns what you tried to do last night to his cousin's child? Ruby came to you for help, and this is how you treat her. She foolishly trusted you, but will never make that mistake again."

Vyne wet his lips. "Clement doesn't need to know."

"Really? Do you imagine I have any reason to keep your dirty secrets from Clement? He is my brother."

Vyne swallowed. "I wasn't sending the child back to Scotland."

"Then where were you sending him?"

"My sister lives alone in Dorset. She's an interest in children."

"So you would break Ruby's heart just to purify the family tree of an offspring of undesirable origins?" Hector nearly shouted.

Vyne held out one hand. "I knew she'd never willingly send the boy away. If the boy were to disappear one night, Ruby would have been able to plead ignorance honestly when her father brought her father-in-law to take him back. Without the child, there'd be no reason for Roper to linger long. He'd have no further connection to my family, or to her. It would be as if the marriage had never happened!"

Hector narrowed his eyes, unable to believe that tall tale. "And then what would have become of the child? Would he grow up imagining his mother had abandoned him?"

"No!" Vyne exclaimed. "I would send her to the child when I was sure Roper had given up hope. I sent a letter ahead to my sister, explaining the situation already. My sister would have taken good care of the boy until her mother came for him."

"And this business with Blackwood? Why were you trying so hard to match Ruby to him?"

"Everyone believes Blackwood needs a wife. He is a wealthy man and has a connection to a title hardly anyone talks about. But I believe he will most likely become a marquis in the not-too-distant future. My daughters are too innocent to appeal to such a man, but with Ruby returned a widow, I saw an opportunity to make a good match for her, little knowing Blackwood's so-called unencumbered life was a lie."

Vyne told a fairly convincing tale. He had painted his motives in a brighter light than might actually be possible. Some of it might even be true if not for one glaring embellishment. He pointed a finger at the earl. "No carriage or horse has left The Vyne's carrying any letter for anyone. I know because I've spent every day watching the front drive."

Lord Vyne paled as Hector advanced on him.

"You will not attempt to make another match for Ruby. You will not concern yourself with her again, or with Pip. From this moment on, you will leave them alone."

"Roper will come to take the boy, and there is nothing she can do to stop him."

Hector would stop Roper. He would find a way to keep mother and son together, no matter what it cost him. "Lord Vyne, I encourage you to spend your solitude contemplating the difference between what is right and what is good for the sake of the family. Perhaps if you think very hard, you might one day see how you are responsible for the state of your empty life." He turned away from Vyne, disgusted with the earl.

Vyne got to his feet. "Where are you going?"

"I'm going to do a good thing."

Vyne was suddenly at Hector's side,

clutching his arm. "What are you going to tell Clement?"

Hector shook him off and Vyne staggered for the support of the wall. "I'll have to think about that," Hector warned, but he would probably tell Clement everything once he had Ruby and Pip safely away from The Vynes. But first… "Do you know what might help me decide?"

"What?"

"Give back the silver bell you took from Ruby when she was a girl. I know you took it from her and allowed *me* to be blamed."

Vyne jerked back from him. "I don't know what you're talking about."

Would Vyne deny every accusation aimed his way? "Thanks to my friendship with your son, I recall the contents of your father's will were hotly contested by you and your brother. Clement told me your father had left little tokens to each of his grandchildren. You argued against honoring the bequests, but your brother won, and you've hardly spoken to him since. You took back that silver bell from Ruby out of spite for your brother's success. She misses it still."

Lord Vyne's eyes lowered, revealing his guilt.

"Your father gave it to *her*, not you."

Vyne's jaw worked then he yanked open a drawer nearby. Inside were a collection of small trinkets, and he removed Ruby's long-lost silver bell.

When he thrust it toward Hector, he refused to take it. "Don't be such a coward.

Give it back to her yourself, and maybe she'll forgive you for what you tried to do one day."

"What about our bargain?"

"I made no bargain with you, but I have the truth of you now."

Hector stalked upstairs and returned to his bedchamber immediately. He'd fetch Pip and take him to Ruby ahead of their departure from the estate.

But he found Ruby and Pip together already, surrounded by Hector's packed trunks. Pip was playing with his horse behind one, and Ruby was seated before the fire.

He turned to Pip first to say good morning. Hector leaned down and ruffled the boy's hair. "Come and sit with your mother and I."

He turned away, sure the boy would follow eventually, and claimed a spot by Ruby's side on a cozy settee. "Good morning."

"I woke to find you gone."

"Yes, I went to speak to your uncle about the abduction attempt."

"Why?"

"Because during the night, I realized it couldn't have been Roper behind it."

Ruby's eyes flickered around the room nervously. "Pip, come and sit with us."

The boy got to his feet and dropped into the space between them. He looked up at Hector and smiled. "Will you take me to visit the horses?"

"Indeed, I will." He ruffled the boy's hair again. "How would you like to visit London for a few days?"

"London?" both Ruby and Pip cried out in surprise.

"Yes, but if we don't run into Clement I'd like to divert to spend Christmas night in my home. I find I have a few extra presents to acquire this year, too, and I have a special license to arrange."

At the word presents, Pip's eyes lit up wide, and he inhaled, anticipating a surprise. Hector hoped his ultimate gift for the boy, a pony, would be enough to wait for.

Ruby touched his arm. "You were serious last night?"

"Every word. I will marry you, and I will deal with the Ropers, and we will make a home for all of us together wherever you'd like to live."

The boy turned to him. "Will you be my new papa?"

"If you want me to be." Hector smiled.

The boy chewed his lower lip.

"I'll teach you to ride as well as your papa and me. I've a friend who keeps a pony in London. We could visit him after I marry your mother."

The boy suddenly wrapped his arms about Hector's neck and hugged him tightly. "Can we go now? I don't like it here."

Hector pulled the boy onto his lap. He leaned down to the boy's ear to whisper but turned his gaze on Ruby. "We could go today, but first, I'd like to have your mama agree to marry me."

"Mama?"

"Yes, Pip."

"Why won't you marry Hector?"

"Well, I suppose I won't marry him because he hasn't asked me," she admitted.

Hector grunted in surprise. He had thought he'd made his interest clear, but perhaps it hadn't been the perfect proposal after all. He could do better.

He lifted the boy off his lap and stood. "May I have your undivided attention, madam?"

"Of course, Lord Stockwick," Ruby promised, fluttering her lashes demurely.

"Well, my dear," he began. "It seems I've found and fallen for the prettiest lady in all of England, and I would like her to be my wife without delay, if she will have me."

He fell to one knee before Ruby and extended his hand to her. She tossed her head slightly from side to side and then burst into the most remarkable smile he'd ever beheld. "Yes. Yes, I would be honored to be your wife, good sir."

Hector shuffled closer. "Darling."

He cupped her face and, after a pause, pulled her in to kiss softly. When he drew back, Pip's face was inches away from them. So the boy didn't feel left out, he kissed his forehead, and then laughed. "I always thought that would be much harder."

Ruby laughed. "It isn't, not when there is love."

"So very true. I swear you'll never feel alone again," Hector promised as he gently wrapped his fingers around her nape. "I'll love you more than you've ever dreamed possible, too. Forever and ever and ever."

Ruby kissed him, and he didn't think there had been a better start to Christmas in all his life. He also predicted Christmas would become his favorite time of year from this moment on. He'd make sure of it.

Epilogue

Ruby set her hands to her hips. "Where do you think you are going, young man?"

Pip froze, his hand inches from the door latch. "I just wanted to look."

"I told you we had to stay here and wait for the carriage to be brought round. It's much too cold to leave the door open."

She gazed at the numerous trunks spread around them in The Vynes' hall and winced that none of them were hers. But their first stop would be the nearest town on the way to Cornwall, where Hector had promised they'd spend the night and go shopping for what Ruby and Pip needed most.

After what Hector had told her of his conversation with Lord Vyne, she couldn't wait to escape her uncle's home. Of all the treacherous, backhanded schemes to help her. Only her family could break her heart and expect her to be grateful.

Only Hector and his valet, Parker, were to be trusted with her son's protection from this moment on.

An odd creak sounded behind her, and she turned slightly.

"So you are leaving without a word of farewell, just like all the rest," Lord Vyne accused.

Ruby considered ignoring her uncle, but

she had been brought up to show respect for elders, even if they were evil. "It seemed appropriate."

She turned fully, finding her uncle being rolled into the room by a servant in a wheeled chair. He looked to have aged a decade in just one night.

"If you're going, I suppose you'll be needing this." He deposited a silver bell onto one of Hector's traveling trunks nearest him.

Ruby frowned as she recognized it.

Her uncle had stolen her silver bell!

Vyne nodded. "You don't belong here, and neither does that anymore."

He had his man roll him away.

Ruby rushed forward and snatched up her precious heirloom. The bell was just as she remembered, engraved with her initials upon the inside. She held it tight to her chest, her eyes misting with tears just as Hector returned. "I've said goodbye to Blackwood for us all. He's finally been repaid and is eager to leave today, too."

Ruby looked around them at the emptiness of The Vynes and sighed. "This will be a lonely place to spend Christmas."

"He brought it all entirely upon himself." He squinted at her hand. "What have you there?"

Ruby lifted her bell and gave it a little shake.

"Ah, I see Vyne saw the wisdom of returning your possession."

"When did you realize he had taken it?"

"The same time I realized he was behind

the attempt to abduct Pip. If he could stoop so low, there was nothing he wouldn't have tried to get away with before."

"He gave it back because of you. Thank you."

Hector's eyes softened. "We should be going. I suspect if I don't marry you quickly enough, I fear I might miss my chance to be Pip's new papa."

"Never fear. You are just the man for the job," she swore.

He was a good man, wonderful with Pip, and she couldn't have chosen better if she'd tried. She raised her little bell high and shook it again. The much-missed twinkle of sound made her so happy. "Come along, Lord Stockwick, we have a Christmas adventure to embark on, and I mean to start it today."

She took Pip's hand and led him out of The Vynes to the carriage. Hector followed, directing servants to load the trunks securely. When he joined them inside the comfortable interior, Pip jumped quickly onto his lap and started peppering the poor man with questions.

Never once on that first day together did Ruby feel Hector regretted the impending loss of his bachelorhood. And after he'd spoiled Ruby with a pretty new gown and cloak, and Pip with toys and even more warm clothing, they took lodgings at a cozy inn, where they spent the night reading the scandalous entries in his journal, highly censored to protect the innocent ears of her young son.

For the first time in a good long while,

Ruby was at last happy and safe and felt loved again. Liam, she felt sure, was looking down on them from above, holding mistletoe over their heads.

———

Thank you reading SILVER BELLS! I hope you enjoyed Hector and Ruby's romance.

Distinguished Rogues Series

Book 1: Chills (FREE READ)
The rogue she can't have is the only one she wants.

Book 2: Broken
His wicked ways could be the best hope for her future.

Book 3: Charity
Reclaiming the love of his life is bound to break a few rules.

Book 4: An Accidental Affair
Being good was a damned nuisance!

Book 5: Keepsake
The runaway bride is back to cause trouble!

Book 6: An Improper Proposal
Educating the innocent might have been a mistake.

Book 7: Reason to Wed
Duty is the last thing on his mind once they kiss.

More Regency Romance...

Wild Randalls Series
Book 1: Engaging the Enemy
Book 2: Forsaking the Prize
Book 3: Guarding the Spoils
Book 4: Hunting the Hero

Saints and Sinners Series
Book 1: The Duke and I
Book 2: A Gentleman's Vow
Book 3: An Earl of Her Own
Book 4: The Lady Tamed

Rebel Hearts Series
Book 1: The Wedding Affair
Book 2: An Affair of Honor
Book 3: The Christmas Affair
Book 4: An Affair so Right

Miss Mayhem Series
Book 1: Miss Watson's First Scandal
Book 2: Miss George's Second Chance
Book 3: Miss Radley's Third Dare
Book 4: Miss Merton's Last Hope

...and many more

About Heather Boyd

USA Today Bestselling Author Heather Boyd believes every character she creates deserves their own happily-ever-after—no matter how much trouble she puts them through. With that goal in mind, she writes steamy romances that skirt the boundaries of propriety to keep readers enthralled until the wee hours of the morning. Heather has published over 40 regency romance novels and shorter works full of daring seductions and distinguished rogues. She lives north of Sydney, Australia, with her trio of rogues and pair of four-legged overlords.

Let's be friends! Find Heather at:
Heather-Boyd.com

facebook.com/HeatherBoydRomanceAuthor

twitter.com/Heather_Boyd

instagram.com/iheatherboyd

bookbub.com/authors/heather-boyd

goodreads.com/Heather_Boyd